SHADOW C

Book 1 of the Misfit Ma

C. S. Churton & Keira Stone

Other Titles By C.S Churton

Druid Academy Series
DRUID MAGIC
FERAL MAGIC
PRIMAL MAGIC

Druid Enforcer Academy Series
FAMILIAR MAGIC

Fur 'n' Fang Academy Series
MOON BITTEN
CURSE BITTEN
FERAL BITTEN

Misfit Magic Academy Series
SHADOW CHARMED
SHADOW CURSED

TalentBorn Series
AWAKENING
EXILED
DEADLOCK
UNLEASHED
HUNTED
CHIMERA

Chapter One

I'm going to make them listen.

That thought repeated on a loop in the back of my mind the entire trip to the Circle. There was no way they could deny my request in person. I mean, sure, they'd basically done it by some stupid letter, but I would change their minds. I had to. There was just no other reasonable outcome to my situation.

All my life I'd known I wasn't as good as my brother. Everyone around me, Mum and Dad especially, never let me forget it. '*Oh, look at how skilled Micah is with magic. What a natural. Oh, did you hear about his manifestation event?*' Even now, with him sitting in a cell awaiting trial, people still whispered about him. About how powerful he must be, what a danger he was. But I could pick out the notes of admiration in their voices. No one ever looked at me that way. No one ever said, '*Wow, Norah has really shown some skill. I can't wait to see what she does next.*' Nope, no one has ever given a damn about me.

Living in Micah's shadow had been a lonely place, not least of all because of how wide his reach extended. I could have been Queen of the World, slinging the most perfect spells around, and no one would have cared. So, I stopped caring, too. The moment I'd decided it wasn't worth my time trying to compete with him, I'd almost felt a weight lift from my shoulders. The albatross of my magic was the last piece to freeing myself completely.

The Circle's headquarters squatted in the distance, the wrought-iron gates topped with menacing points standing as a reminder that the druids were the ones in charge. What they said stood as the law of the land. When I'd stopped giving a damn about being as good as Micah, let alone better than him, I'd realised that it was better to not even have magic. And so, I'd sent off my request that they bind my powers. They hadn't even spelled my name right in their short, form rejection.

I'd stuffed the letter in my back pocket and pulled it out now as the cabbie trundled along the road. It was amazing how small you could make something just by folding it into quarters. Not that they even needed that much paper for their response. Unfolding it like I was undoing origami, I stared at the printed text, rereading the words I'd committed to memory since it had arrived a week ago.

To Nora Sheehan,

We have received your request regarding the binding of your magical ability. At this time, we are denying your request. We will not consider any further requests.

There was an ornate circle seal at the bottom. They couldn't even be bothered to sign their own names. Just another way to make us all feel beneath them. The pad of my right index finger rubbed against the raised wax and I noted the subtle design of the circle itself. It was made of tiny interlocking links that you wouldn't notice if you didn't pay close attention.

The cold, detached wording of their statement only fanned the flames of my desire to be rid of the power within me. They might have said they wouldn't reconsider, but I was going to make them. No one should have to be saddled with powers they didn't want. Especially if it meant I'd finally had something to separate me from Micah.

"We're here, miss," the driver said, glancing over his shoulder at me impatiently.

He was probably irritated that he had to come this far out of the city to get me here with no promise of a fare back the other way. I contemplated asking him to wait but I had no idea how long my grovelling would take, and I wasn't in any mood to be out of pocket more than necessary.

"Yeah, uh thanks," I mumbled and stuffed the letter into my front pocket, not caring if I crumpled it into an unreadable mess.

The engine rumbled as he sat there waiting for me to pay and get the hell out of the car. I cast a quick glance at the meter still ticking away and cringed inwardly at the fact I was out nearly forty quid for the trip. *Bloody highway robbery, that is.* I forked over a fistful of ten-pound notes and slid out of the backseat without bothering to ask for change.

To no one's surprise, the cab beat a hasty retreat back down the road and left me standing outside the gates. Beyond them, the building itself looked rundown and derelict, like some long-abandoned manor house. The front door hung off its hinges at an odd angle, and one of the windows looked like it had been smashed. A sliver of doubt gnawed at me. Had I come to the right place? Was anyone even here? I glanced back over my shoulder, but the cab was long gone. There was no turning back. I twisted back round and stared through the gates again. It wasn't at all how I'd imagined the building that housed the most powerful magical council in the country. The gates themselves, though, they were exactly what I'd expected. The harsh, brushed metal seemed even more imposing up close, and I had no clue how I was supposed to gain entry. I didn't see any guards or even a buzzer to announce my presence. No way was I going to just stand there and hope someone took pity on me—assuming anyone was even here. I pressed the palm of my right hand against the bar nearest to me and gave it a solid shove inward.

To my surprise, the gate swung open on silent hinges.

I should have picked up on the oddity of the fact it was so easy to enter the grounds. From everything I knew about the Circle, they hated people showing up on their doorstep unannounced. Admittedly, that being my exact plan wasn't the most well-thought out of ideas. But, as I'd been repeating since I got into the back of the cab: I was going to make them listen.

A brisk autumn wind whipped around me, tugging at loose strands of my muddy brown hair. If I looked closely, I could still see the last vestiges of the dark purple I'd introduced over the summer to make it stand out. Mum had nearly massacred me for the stunt. I'd been floored she'd even noticed. The breeze caressed my cheek, and I couldn't help leaning into it, as if it were a physical person offering me a moment of comfort. As if to say, "I see you, Norah". If all went well, no one would have to see me again unless I chose to be seen.

I took a step forward onto the grounds and a shiver that had nothing to do with the gust of wind tap-danced down my spine, hitting every vertebra individually. Another step onward and my hands ached as if I'd stuck them in a freezer for too long. I glanced down at my right hand and for a split second I swore I saw a thin ribbon of a cut where my skin had touched metal. A single droplet of blood pooled in my now-cupped palm. *What the hell?*

I blinked, and the droplet vanished. The ache

subsided and I filed it away as just a weird bout of nerves. The Circle wouldn't have booby trapped their own entrance. *Right?*

"Get a grip," I chided myself and squared my shoulders—and then blinked in shock. I wasn't staring at a derelict manor house anymore. The building in front of me was much bigger than the one I'd seen from outside the gates. It didn't just *seem* bigger—it literally wasn't the same building. This one was made of immaculate grey stone and stood several stories high. Tall spires adorned either end of the mansion…or maybe castle was a better description. The broken door had been replaced with an imposing, thick oaken slab, and the windows were tall and sombre, and not a single one of them was smashed.

It must have been a glamour—a way to keep the mundanes, and anyone else they didn't like the look of, from seeing what was lying behind their warded gates. A way to keep us lesser mortals away. Well, it wasn't working. Not today.

Marching across the sprawling circular drive to the headquarters proper felt like it took an eon to traverse. Leave it to the bigwigs to flaunt their status and power in the most patriarchal way possible. Finally, the treads of my shoes hit the sleek marble of the front steps and it was all I could to avoid face planting on them when I took them at too eager a gait.

Steadying myself against the front door, I glanced around to be sure no one had witnessed the near embarrassment. Of course, there was no one to see me. I took a minute to collect my composure and yanked on the heavy oaken door before me. Unlike the gate, the door fought against being opened. I had to put my shoulder into it, and it groaned like an angry old man being ushered along, irritated at having to do something for someone else.

The interior foyer felt like it belonged in a cathedral with its vaulted ceilings and arches. I even spotted a few bits of stained glass high up where the light would catch it in the evening, turning the space a kaleidoscope of colours. It would be beautiful, but I didn't have time to dwell on that. I needed to find an actual member of the Circle and plead my case to them. They had to understand why I didn't want this burden anymore. I had to believe that the human interaction, having to look me in the eye, would do the trick.

There was no helpful signage to direct me saying 'pompous druids second door on the right' so I had to cast about. It gave me an excuse to study the rest of the building and note that whatever I might think of the people in power, someone back along their line had damned good taste in interior decorating. There were heavy tapestries adorning the wall directly to my left depicting magical battles. My fingers trembled, and I glanced over my shoulder before pressing the pads of my fingers to the threads. I could feel each individual strand woven together to create the whole. I'd never experienced anything like it. I half-expected it to burst into flame or electrocute me, but nothing happened. Except I left oily fingerprint residue on a who-knew-how-old tapestry.

Wandering in the other direction, I found what looked like a library with an empty fireplace and bookshelves with carefully arranged and preserved texts. My curiosity getting the better of me yet again, I eased a slender volume off a low shelf. The publication date told me it was a first edition from 1901. I quickly returned it to its place and shuffled out of the room. The library appeared to be the main attraction on this floor, so I made my way up the single winding staircase, tromping up far too many flights before finding a landing. I looked down at the way I'd come, and my stomach sloshed. I wasn't afraid of heights, but it was a long way down.

My brain wanted to call where I'd ended up the second floor, but given how many stairs I'd trudged up, it had to be higher than that. Plus, the exterior had looked to be at least five or six stories. The lighting up here was dimmer, and it was clear there were smaller gathering spaces, little alcoves with chintzy reading lamps with those ridiculous green glass shades. I stopped in the middle of the corridor and tried to sense any magic around me. But given that I'd never actually manifested a unique power, it didn't surprise me that I couldn't pick up on whether there was any actively in use around me. A pang of disappointment lanced through my chest, stealing my breath away. I'd come here to get rid of any connection to magic. It was exactly what I wanted and here I was feeling sorry that I couldn't pick up on it. *What was wrong with me?*

Not wanting to lose my nerve, I started opening every door I came across. Each was empty and of no use to me. Just when I was about to give up, retrace my steps, and retreat down the spiral staircase of nausea, I spotted a door standing ajar at the very far end of the corridor. I thought I'd gone all the way down that end, but I must have missed one.

All the doors were beginning to blur together. I nudged this new door open with my toe and peered inside. It was warmly lit with more natural lighting than any of the other rooms I'd seen. A single mahogany desk sat in one corner and there was a second door on the opposite wall. What it concealed was anyone's guess. I wasn't stupid enough to try it. If it was this far secreted away, there was a logical reason for it.

I spied a white China teacup with a pale grey-blue accent along the rim and handle nestled in a delicate silver saucer on the desk. A quick examination revealed the contents were still warm. Not piping hot, but room temperature. Its owner hadn't been gone long. Maybe they'd popped off to the loo. There was a single hardbacked chair pressed up against the far wall and I thought about sitting down. It offered an unobstructed view of the exterior door so I wouldn't be taken by surprise when Miss—or Mister—Tea Drinker returned.

The unnerving shiver that had followed my entry onto the ground returned, this time with an uncomfortable prickling of the tiny hairs on the nape of my neck. Like I was being watched. I detested that sensation. Even if I could have a good view of the door, I decided against sitting down. Instead, I paced back and forth, reciting my argument in my head for why the Circle needed to grant my request.

"You see, I've never shown that much magical aptitude. And it's safer for everyone if I just don't have magic. That way no one has to worry about another Micah incident."

If I framed it as a public safety consideration, maybe that would appeal to their sense of justice. What my brother had done was unspeakable, and I didn't disagree that he deserved to be locked up and tried for his crimes. Not that anyone ever asked me what I thought. All they saw was the lesser Sheehan child, the one who could never live up to *his* legacy. Good or bad.

"You're not supposed to be here."

Her voice yanked me from my internal monologue, and I spun to see a young red-headed woman standing in the doorway. She didn't look surprised to see me.

"Uh, sorry?" I murmured, taking an involuntary step backward, my calf brushing against the front of the chair directly behind me.

"You're not supposed to be here," she repeated.

Well, shit.

Chapter Two

"How did you get onto the grounds?"

Her brow creased, and her breathy voice was tinged with a mix of curiosity and concern. I figured I'd better answer quickly before concern won out and landed me in a dungeon or something.

"No one said I couldn't come in," I offered lamely and made a vague gesture toward the exterior of the building.

She pursed her lips, smoothed a crease in her trousers, and took a step closer. I started to reach for the letter crumpled in my back pocket, but stopped abruptly. I didn't want her to think I was reaching for a weapon and do whatever it was druids did to people who crossed them. *Like locking them up in high security prisons for months awaiting trial.*

"Well, someone should have. You, um, you can't be here without permission." She glanced around the room. Was she…*nervous?* "And definitely not in *this* room. Did someone summon you?"

"Um, not exactly." I reached for my pocket again, and when she didn't stop me, pulled out the letter.

She stepped forward and plucked it out of my hand, smoothing the crinkled edges to read it. Either she was a really slow reader, or she was trying to find a polite way to tell me to sod off because she studied the paper for a solid five minutes in silence. Her gaze flickered across the text, darting upwards more than a few times. Like she was checking something.

"You really shouldn't have come," she finally said. "The council were very clear in their judgement."

"I know, but if they just give me five minutes, I can make them see…" I began, but she held up a hand.

"And this doesn't explain how an unclassified got onto the grounds without permission."

She arched a brow at me, and I scuffed my feet. I knew I shouldn't let the term unclassified bother me, and yet it still stung. It was another reminder that we were less than other people. Different.

"Um…through the front gate?" I said, avoiding her eye. I mean, it was the truth. I could feel her searching my face, and then she seemed to reach a decision.

"You should come with me."

She reached a hand out towards my arm and I jerked it away, taking a hurried step back.

"You're not in any danger from me," she said, and try as I might to focus on the first part of that statement, I couldn't help but get hung up on the 'from me' part. "Still, it would be better if you weren't found inside the office of Senior Councilman Hutton."

She gave me a conspiratorial smile, and added, "For

both of us."

She gestured to the door, and I stepped through without arguing. If this druid was afraid of whoever this office belonged to—and it seemed like she was—then it was a fair bet I didn't want to meet them.

The druid fell into step beside me, her ridiculous red cloak fanning out behind her as she walked. She didn't attempt to touch me again, and that was probably the reason I didn't object. I would, however, very much have liked to know where we were going. I opened my mouth to ask, but she beat me to it.

"Can I ask why you would want to bind your powers?" she said as she handed back the letter. I crumpled it back into my pocket without looking at it.

"I don't expect someone like you to understand," I said.

"Try me," she challenged, lifting her chin.

I studied the defiant look on her face, and something about her, something I couldn't quite pinpoint, made me think of my brother. But that didn't make sense. Maybe I was just too used to seeing that same touch of arrogance on his face—but arrogance wasn't a trait reserved solely for him.

"I don't have much in the way of magical talent," I said, trying to shake the unsettling feeling. "I mean, I had to sit a test to see if I even had magic."

"Sitting tests isn't that uncommon," she said. "And just because you had to sit the test doesn't mean you should want to bind your magic. Have you started at Braeseth Academy yet?"

I snorted. "You mean the misfit magic academy? No, I haven't started there yet." I turned my gaze to the smooth stones beneath our feet.

"Then how can you be sure that binding your magic is the right move?"

"Because I can't miss what I've never had," I replied, as we turned left round a corner.

"We're the lucky ones," she said. "We have the power in us to do great things. I know it might seem scary, and believe me, I do understand what it's like to have something inside you that you don't think you can control."

"Yeah, sure," I huffed, battling the urge to roll my eyes. The only thing it looked like she struggled to control was the frizzy red hair tied back behind her head. She gave me a small smile that caught me off guard. Why was she being so nice?

"Let's just say there was a time I was afraid of the power within me, but I've conquered that fear. It's part of me, whether I asked for it or not. I'm sure you'll feel the same if you let yourself explore what your own power holds, if you just give it a chance."

15

I tried not to let her get into my head. I'd come here with a distinct purpose and I wasn't leaving until I had the outcome I wanted. I could still sense a strange bit of Micah in her voice that made no sense. It had to be a coincidence or something. I couldn't just ask this perfect stranger if she'd ever met or spent time with my brother. That would be too presumptuous, and she'd assume I was just as arrogant as him. Even so, Micah and I had spent enough time together for me to pick up on some of his energies, and this woman was giving them off in an eerily similar fashion. Then again, though I'd spent most of my time trying to figure out how to be as good as him, I didn't exactly pay attention to the specifics of what he did.

"You're not going to convince them to change their minds, you know," she said, almost apologetically.

"You don't know that," I insisted.

"Well, it's true I haven't worked here very long, and maybe you're right," she said, though I got the sense she was just humouring me. "But I've listened to how they operate. If they decree something, they don't change it just because someone shows up and puts a face to a name on a letter. I've never seen them reverse a decision like that."

"Come on…" I trailed off, realising that she knew my name because she'd read the letter, but I didn't have so much as a name tag to guess at hers.

"Kelsey," she said, almost as if she'd read my mind.

I nodded. "Come on, Kelsey. Can't you help a girl out? I mean, it's great you embraced your power or whatever, but I don't want this. I didn't ask to be a witch and frankly, I've been rubbish at it so far. Everyone would be happier if I just could go live a normal life where they didn't have to acknowledge my presence."

Kelsey gave me a sympathetic look as she steered us round another corner and down a staircase. "Believe me, I know it feels insurmountable, but I really think you can get a handle on it if you just give it a chance. You must be due to start at Braeseth soon?"

"Not if I have any say in it." What was the point of attending a school for magic if I didn't want to use my magic? But, as I looked across at her, a thought planted itself in my mind. "What if you did it?"

She blinked at me. "Did what?"

"Bound my magic. We wouldn't have to bother the Circle about it. I mean, it can't be that hard, right?"

Kelsey's cheeks burned bright, and she ducked her head to avoid looking at me. "Not that I'm not flattered, but that's not how binding works. Binding requires consent of the whole council and has to be performed by the Head Councilman himself."

I could tell there was more of an explanation than she

was letting on. Was her magic incompatible with mine? Was that even a thing? Pushing those questions aside, I gnawed my lower lip and tried again. "Couldn't we bend the rules just this once?" I put on my best pouty lips and gave her wide, innocent eyes.

Her smile had an edge of pity in it that rubbed me the wrong way. "I'm sorry, but we can't. The rules are there for a reason. It's not just me or the rest of the council they're here to protect. If anyone could go around binding anyone else's powers, can you imagine the chaos it would cause?"

We reached the end of the corridor and it split off in two directions. I got the feeling one of those directions—the one Kelsey was looking down right now—would lead to the exit. I was running out of time, and I couldn't blow this. I wouldn't get another chance.

"I guess I could see how that would cause a problem," I agreed, dragging my feet to a halt and turning to meet her eye. "But I'm not asking you to go around binding magic all over the show. Just me, here, right now."

"You must think I'm pretty powerful," she murmured.

I waved my hands around to indicate the fancy building we both found ourselves in. "You do work here, Kelsey."

The bright embarrassed splotches on her cheeks darkened. "Only as an apprentice. I don't have the kind of power you'd need. It has to be done by someone with more power than the person they're binding."

"Even an apprentice would have more magic than me. Hell, your shoes probably have more magic than me," I glowered.

"I'm sorry. Really, I am. I can see that this is really hard for you, but it has to be the council who performs the spell."

I wanted to tell her that she was wrong. That there had to be another way around this stupid rule. Why would they make it so only they had this authority? Didn't their leaders know how to delegate? But I kept that criticism to myself. She clearly liked her job here, and so far she'd seemed pretty nice. I wasn't about to risk that kindness when I apparently wasn't even supposed to be on the grounds in the first place.

"They must listen to you, though. They can't just ignore you completely if you're training under them," I blurted.

Kelsey sighed. "I wish that were true. But I'm afraid it doesn't work that way."

"I don't need you to convince them to do anything other than just listen to me. Don't they owe me that? They didn't even give me a real explanation as to why they won't entertain my request." I gestured to my pocket where the letter was stowed. "You read what they wrote. I mean, it sounds like they didn't even seriously consider it in the first place. And is it so hard for them to double check how someone spells their name?" The last bit came out in a rush of words before I realised I'd said them.

She snorted, then tried to cover it up by coughing into her hand. Her expression grew serious, and she nodded. "Okay. I'll speak to them, but I can't make any promises."

"Thank you. That's all I'm asking for," I said.

She turned and steered us down the corridor in the opposite direction of where I assumed the exit lay, and her step was more purposeful, so that I had to hurry to keep up, though the faster pace seemed to come more easily to her. She noticed me falling behind, flushed red, and slowed her pace again. A moment later, we reached the end of the winding hallway and found ourselves staring at a large oak door that had to be an easy fifteen feet tall, and wide enough for four people to enter abreast. The hinges alone were as big as my hands.

"Please wait here," she said, and raised a hand to rap on the door. It swung open a fraction and she slipped inside, and then it slammed shut behind her, and a blue glow shimmered across its surface, which, unless I was very much mistaken, was some sort of magic lock.

I had no idea why she'd want to lock herself in with them, but maybe it was more about locking me out. I couldn't blame her. I'd barged in unannounced and wandered the halls, likely more than she knew. Or had she been the one watching me from the shadows, waiting to see where I ended up? She'd mentioned having power she'd been afraid of.

I stood there trying to decide what sort of power Kelsey possessed for what felt like ages. Maybe that was what this place did to you. It elongated time to such an absurd degree that you got pissed off and abandoned your goals. Well, it wasn't going to work on me. I had no plans to leave this hallway until I'd talked to someone with the title Senior Council Member. I envisioned them all in long, flowing hooded robes of midnight blue or black. The kind that obscured their faces just to make them seem more powerful and mysterious. That seemed like something the governing body of our world would do. Or maybe I'd just been fed too many silly fairytales as a child.

I stared idly at a series of flickering torches hanging near the ceiling, and then realised what I was seeing. They weren't torches, they were fireballs, seemingly sustaining themselves as they cast light in the hallway without setting anything on fire, or giving off so much as a smudge of smoke. I snorted to myself. Typical arrogant druids, throwing magic around like it was nothing.

I drummed my fingers on my thighs, tapping out a simple four count at first before transitioning into a more complex beat with mixed rhythms. I was so lost in the rat-tat-tat-rat, I didn't notice the blue shimmer vanish from the door until it swung open, and Kelsey stepped through.

"They've agreed to see you," she said. Her cheeks looked flushed, and I caught the slight sheen of sweat on her brow.

Logically, I knew I wasn't out of the woods yet. But she'd given me a compass and pointed me north, so I felt like I owed her something. A hug was too personal, and we'd only just met. So I wiped my hands on my jeans, and held one out to her.

"Thanks for convincing them to hear me out."

She eyed my outstretched hand warily for a second before shaking it. Her skin had a roughness to it that suggested she'd spent a lot of time outdoors. Or digging in the earth. A botanist, perhaps?

"Try not to get your hopes up," she said with another of those sad smiles. "I doubt they're going to change their minds."

"Leave that to me," I said, trying to project confidence and strength. In truth, I was starting to doubt my plan all together. But here went nothing.

She touched her hand to the door and it opened—I assumed with magic, because she hadn't touched it *that* hard—and gestured for me to enter in front of her. Once I crossed the threshold, the door closed itself, and though I didn't look back, I was sure the blue glow was back, locking me inside.

Kelsey clamped one hand onto my shoulder to guide me forward, and this time I didn't object to the physical contact.

We were standing inside a circular room—clichéd, much—that was bigger than any other room I'd been in, even at my old high school. It was fancier, too. The entire lower half of the walls was wooden panelling, and the upper half was made of some sort of stone that seemed to shine, like someone had dug out the centre of a quarry and polished it until it had a mirror finish.

Polished wooden benching sat all the way round the curved walls, except for a gap directly opposite the door, where the largest courtroom bench I'd ever seen squatted, presiding over the entire room. Sitting behind it was a grey-haired man who could only be the Head Councilman, and scattered throughout the room, the other council members. I'd got my wish.

The Head Councilman's gaze bored into me and I tried not to flinch. I hadn't expected to actually talk to all of them. Maybe one or two. Something far more manageable and that made me feel less on trial. Kelsey nudged me forward with a light shove between my shoulder blades. I glanced at her and she gave me a discreet thumbs-up but made no effort to leave. She was staying and in some small way, that gave me a confidence boost.

"Speak, or leave," the Head Councilman said, his voice booming and echoing in the space around.

"My name is Norah Sheehan," I started, but he held up his hand to silence me.

"We know who you are. We know why you are here. Were you unable to read our prior response?"

I'm perfectly literate, you arsehole.

I set my jaw and counted to five in my head before answering. "Yes, I can read. But, sir, your letter didn't exactly contain much detail about why you denied my request." My voice was barely loud enough to echo back at me.

He glanced around at his colleagues and low murmurs filled the space. Had no one ever questioned one of their directives before? "And I thought, perhaps I wasn't clear enough in explaining why I wanted my powers bound in the first place," I pushed on.

"You've said enough," the Head Councilman answered, glaring down at me. "We do not owe you any more explanation than was already provided."

I caught one of the women down the far-left side giving him a disapproving look. Maybe I had started with the wrong tactic by trying to appeal to the head of the organisation. Maybe I needed to reach out to the lower-level members. If I got enough of them on my side, even all of them, surely the Head Councilman couldn't go against the wishes of everyone else? But I couldn't let that arrogant wanker get away with speaking to me like that.

"No offence meant, but, if you were just going to tell me to piss off, why even let me come in here?"

Icy tendrils wrapped around my throat and chest, burning and freezing my lungs and vocal cords at the same time. I couldn't breathe. I couldn't speak. And I had the distinct feeling the Head Councilman was doing this to me.

I really hated magic.

Chapter Three

Time slowed as black spots popped in my vision the longer the magic cut off my oxygen supply. I fought to stay upright and fixed him with what I hoped was a 'fuck you' expression. The woman I'd made eye contact with moments ago waved a hand and the feeling relented.

"She has a point," she said. "Let the girl speak."

That was one person on my side. Time to sway the others to my cause. The Head Councilman's face clouded with annoyance, but he made an exaggerated waving gesture, signalling for me to speak.

"I know I'm a nobody to you all. Believe me, that's been the story of my life. I don't have any special magical abilities. No amount of studying has changed that and after what happened with my brother…" I knew it was risky to bring Micah up, but I needed these people to understand that I wasn't him. "I'm not like him, but I don't want to risk something happening down the road."

"You say you are no one of note, and yet your words portend threat of further violence," he said.

"No. I'm not saying I'm going to do anything. I'm just trying to protect people. Be altruistic. Besides, shouldn't the idea of Micah Sheehan's sister not having powers be a relief to the lot of you?" I arched a brow at him. "I see the way you're looking at me right now. You don't trust me. You think just because I share genetics and a last name that I'm going to be him. Well, before everything happened, I might have agreed with you. But that's not who I am."

I started pacing the length of the room. "I just want to be left alone. I shouldn't have to live with this burden inside me. I didn't ask to be born into a magical family. So, please, do everyone a favour and just bind what magic I have." I'd intended to stop there, but the next words fell out of my mouth as if they had a mind of their own. "You sit up here in your fancy towers, behind layers of closed doors. You want people to listen to you, to respect you and the rules you set. Maybe show some benevolence for once."

"We will take your request under reconsideration," the woman said. She gave Kelsey a curt nod.

"Wait, that's it?" I said. "No, I need you to listen to me. You've got to bind my powers. Now. Please."

"We will take your request under reconsideration," the woman repeated. "Remain outside. We will advise you of our decision."

Kelsey wrapped her hand around my elbow and guided me back through the door. We stopped at the antechamber and I exhaled a long breath.

"So, that could have gone worse."

"No matter what happens, you should be happy with

the fact you made the most powerful governing body in the magic community listen to you. Not many people can say that."

"Yeah, well, let's hold the celebrations until they've finished 'reconsidering'," I murmured.

The relative brightness of the corridor blinded me. I blinked too fast, trying to clear my vision before I made a fool of myself by tripping over something obvious—like my own feet. I took the safe option and leaned back against the wall. I'd done what I could to change their minds. It might not have been the speech of the century, but I'd been honest. That had to count for something.

"Life with magic really won't be that bad," she said.

"Bit pessimistic, aren't you?" I offered.

She chuckled, and I jerked my eyes from the ground to stare at her.

"No-one's ever accused me of being pessimistic before. The opposite, usually. But you should try not to set your expectations too high."

There were no clocks in here, and my watch had stopped working the moment I'd stepped inside, but it felt like a long time passed before I worked up the courage to bring up what was on my mind.

"The Head Councilman, he did something to me to stop me from speaking. I've never felt anything like it before. Cold and burning like fire at the same time." I failed to repress a full-body shiver. "I never want to feel anything like that again."

"He shouldn't have done that," she said, an edge to her voice. She, like the other council member, disagreed with his methods. "It wasn't fair of him to use his power on you like that."

I kept the question of why no one had ousted him from his seat of power to myself. I was making enough waves right now just by being here. "Is that a common thing? He just does that to people?"

She shook her head. "No. He's not a violent man. I think... Honestly, I don't know what he was thinking, and I don't want to speak for him. It's not my place."

It was a copout, but I didn't say anything. Just let my gaze slide off to one side of her. Kelsey opened her mouth to speak, but her head whipped to the side and gaze narrowed on the door.

"They've reached a decision," she announced, turning to approach it.

"How do you...never mind."

We returned to the chamber and, like she'd done before, Kelsey gave me an encouraging look and stood behind me. I faced the council members, trying not to look at the Head Councilman. I didn't know if I could keep my mouth shut if it was bad news and I didn't want him thinking I was being mouthy on purpose.

"Ms Sheehan," the woman who'd seemed to be on my side said, and I turned my attention to her. "We appreciate your petition and the reasons behind it. We also understand that you are young, and you have not yet learned to harness the magic you possess."

"But that's the point," I began, but she held up a hand and I snapped my jaw shut with an audible click.

"No one here wishes to see anything like what happened this past year repeat itself, but I think we also cannot act in such a pre-emptive manner. Frankly, it is not fair to you. You are not your brother, as you say, but you have not been allowed to find out who you are. If we bound everyone's magic simply because of a relation, blood or otherwise, with individuals who break the law, there would be very few people left to practise and learn."

I could already hear the let down in her voice. Somehow, coming from her, it felt like less of a slap in the face. Still, I didn't agree with her assessment. I clasped my hands behind my back, twisting my fingers until my knuckles popped in an effort to keep silent.

"For these reasons, your petition has been denied. And understand that this decision is final. Unless you end up in a courtroom for violation of law which would merit such a punishment," she leaned forward to emphasise her point, "which I pray you do not use as a loophole, this decision cannot be further appealed. Do you understand?"

I swallowed and let out a slow exhale through my nose. "Yes, Ma'am."

"Good."

I pivoted, but the 'ahem' of her clearing her throat stopped me. I looked at her over my shoulder and she made a rotating motion with her pointer finger on her left hand. I reversed course.

"You are expected to attend Braeseth. You may not believe you deserve a chance to hone your skills, but we do." She gave me a small smile before waving me off dismissively. "You may go now."

Kelsey led the way back into the corridor for the second time. I sighed loudly once the door swung shut behind us. My reaction didn't faze Kelsey. She just watched me in silence, and I felt all the fight and energy drain out of me. I scuffed the toe of my shoe against the floorboards.

"You think you can help me get a ride back to the city?"

She beamed at me and bobbed her head.

"I can do one better than that. Come this way."

I cocked my head, but hurried along with her, falling into step beside her as she guided us through several long hallways, and up—not down—a set of stairs.

Eventually, she pushed open a small wooden door

and ushered me inside, shutting it behind us. I glanced around. Nothing about the small room looked remotely like a way out to me, which was probably for the best, because I didn't need to step out of a window and plummet to my death.

"Uh, not to appear ungrateful," I said, "but I wasn't planning a sit-in. They made it pretty clear I'm supposed to get out."

"Just wait here a moment," she said, and hurried over to a cupboard set against one wall. She busied herself rooting through it, and then turned back to me, looking pleased with herself.

She handed me a small stone. I stared at it. The light hit it, flickering through the colour spectrum. "Uh, it's pretty, I guess."

She held up an identical one in her hand. "It's a way to stay in touch. I know you aren't exactly thrilled about going to Braeseth and learning how to use your powers, but I want you to know you're not alone."

I wanted to reject her gift, tell her I didn't need her help or her friendship, but instead I pocketed the stone. "Thanks."

"Don't be afraid of learning everything you can. I promise, it's going to be worth it."

"Uh, should I be worried one of the council is going to hunt me down wanting this back?"

"I'll take care of that. And really, stay in touch. No one should have to feel like they're alone in this world. You may not believe you've got greatness in you, but I have a good feeling about you. I can sense it. You just have to learn to trust it."

Before I could think of anything to say back, she pressed her empty hand to the wall and muttered something too fast and too low for me to catch, though I suspected it wasn't in English. A bright light pulsed from the wall, and then faded out. Kelsey nodded in satisfaction.

"Uh, what was that?"

"A ward," she said. "I've temporarily deactivated it, so we can get you home."

I was about to ask how I was supposed to do that when she stretched out her arm in front of her.

"*Eachlais!*"

A large circle, roughly my height, sprung into existence, like a floating movie screen, and through it I could see my home. I'd only seen portals a couple of times in my life, but there was no mistaking that's what this was. I didn't bother to ask when she'd worked out where I lived.

"Take care, now, Norah," she said. "And try to keep an open mind about Braeseth."

I nodded, having absolutely no intention of doing

that, and stepped towards the portal. I'd go to their stupid academy, but there was no way I was going to actually enjoy it.

Chapter Four

I wasn't sure what I'd expected when I set foot on Braeseth's grounds. I'd been so busy in my youth chasing my brother's shadow, I hadn't paid much attention to what surrounded him. The large complex with only three stories didn't exactly project nobility or notoriety. Dragging my suitcase behind me, I struggled up the front steps and into a modest but unadorned entry hall. Small clusters of teenagers milled about. Some seemed to know each other, but many hugged the perimeter, glancing at their surroundings as if trying to decide whether to blend into the background or stand out.

I started for the far left of the space, picking out a small stretch of wall that was unoccupied when a deep voice called out behind me, "Miss, you need to check in."

I repressed a groan, lugged the suitcase behind me, and shouldered my way through some of the other clusters to a low table set up along the far-right wall. The man who'd called out to me settled back behind the table. He sported a thick blond beard and hair that fell to his shoulders. He had it swept back in a plait. I shifted my weight under his emerald gaze.

"Name?" he prompted; his pen held at the ready, along with a single sheet of paper with names scrawled on it.

35

"Norah Sheehan," I answered softly.

He bent over his list, using the pen to scan the names. "Ah, there you are," he finally said, putting a small tick mark next to my name. "Right. You're in north dorm four."

I thumped my heel against the side of my suitcase. "Any chance I can drop this thing off before whatever else happens? It's kind of heavy." I also noticed that most of the students didn't have theirs with them.

He hooked a thumb over his shoulder with one hand and handed me a placard with my name and the designation N4 on it. "Just stick that on the side and someone will take it up."

That seemed sketchy. I didn't want some stranger rifling through my things. I didn't take the placard that he offered, and after a moment he let out an audible exhale. "You've got your case locked, right?"

"Yeah but, we're at a school for magic. Pretty sure a lock doesn't mean shit to most people," I answered. My cheeks flushed when I realised I'd let the curse slip out.

"I'll personally make sure it gets to your room untouched, all right?" He offered the placard again, and I took it from him, affixing it to the side of the case. "Good. You're welcome to find space in here until the dean brings everyone in for the Start of Semester speech."

"Right. Thanks Mr uh…"

"Instructor Rathbone," he answered, and his eyes sparkled with amusement as he added, "Welcome to Misfits."

"Instructor Rathbone. Right." I coughed to hide my surprise at one of the instructors using the slang name for the academy. "Uh. Thanks."

I set my case next to a few others that had been left along the wall and scurried back across the entry hall. By some miracle the empty space remained, and I slid into it. I pressed myself in as tight as I could. The few people on either side of me didn't seem to pay me any attention. At least not at first. The longer we waited, the more eyes I felt on me.

Murmurs circled around me, but I tried to ignore them, to pretend they weren't whispering about me. No one should even know who I was here. Before I could let the annoyance escalate to panic and send me racing for a dark corner somewhere, the doors to my left opened and an older man with sparse hair wreathing his head just above his ears appeared.

"First year students, please follow me this way." His voice was soft but carried authority. I was sure he was using magic to make his voice louder to get everyone's attention.

The people around me began funnelling through the doors. I stepped through the threshold to find that the room was set up like a theatre with tiered rows of seats in curving formation with a dais at the front.

"Please take a seat," the balding man said as he retreated to the dais.

I found a seat the back—the less people to focus on me—and pulled my knees up to my chest. I tried to pass it off as being nice for anyone else who wanted to get in the row past me. No one else sat in my row. When the doors finally closed, I did a quick headcount. There were maybe fifty of us all told in a room that was able to hold at least twice that many. In all honesty, it looked kind of pathetic.

Down at the front of the room, the man with the thinning hairline shuffled papers on the lectern and cleared his throat. Whatever magic he'd used to project his voice was still working because the sound reverberated against the confined space.

"Good afternoon, everyone," he began. He turned his head slowly in an arc, ostensibly to make some sort of connection with each of us. "My name is Thomas Bevan, and I am the dean here at Braeseth." He paused and I could have sworn his gaze fell right on me. "I am thrilled to have each of you with us this semester."

Yeah, I bet you are.

The rest of the students snickered, but the general rumble died down quickly. Dean Bevan flashed a nervous smile and his head bobbed toward the corners of the room. I craned my neck to see what—or, more accurately, who—he was looking at. There were two people in uniforms and black trimmed cloaks standing at the door and against the far corner. Standing sentinel.

"As this is the first time many of you have graced our halls, I want to establish some simple ground rules as you begin your magical education. There is to be no mixing of dorms."

A flutter of scoffs went up throughout the room. Fan-bloody-tastic. Of course, I'd get stuck with a bunch of randy idiots. Bevan cleared his throat again. "Additionally, please remember that the kitchens close promptly at twenty-two hundred hours. The third floor is also off limits to all students due to…repairs that remain underway."

That comment raised the most feedback from the students around me. None of us had been here last year, but it was no secret that the academy had been attacked. That my brother had been among the ones who'd staged the assault. A small part of me wondered what damage he'd inflicted on the building. But I refused to give into that curiosity. Getting caught out of bounds would get me noticed and that was the opposite of what I wanted. If I had to be here, I was going to fly under the radar.

"Lastly, you will notice druid enforcers on the

grounds. They are here to help clear up the last vestiges of the curse placed on the academy. Please allow them to do their work and treat them with the respect they deserve as guests in our halls."

That explained the two uniforms at the back of the room. The idea of having guards patrolling should have made us feel safer, but the nervous looks on the faces of my classmates suggested it had the opposite effect. Their presence signalled that we were not, in fact, safe here. Had the Circle known that when they insisted I attend?

"Now, as today is Saturday, you will have tomorrow to get acquainted with the grounds and your classmates. Lessons begin promptly Monday morning. You're going to get to know the people sitting around you, as you'll be taking classes with them all year. I am certain you will all become fast friends."

Doubt it.

"I encourage everyone to get settled in their dormitories. We will be offering a welcome supper on the front lawns in an hour. I hope to see you there."

Down in the front, a hand shot up and a red-haired guy nearly leapt from his seat. Dean Bevan pressed his lips into a firm line before relenting and gesturing for the guy to speak.

"Sir, how are we supposed to know how to find our dormitories?"

A few people around him laughed. I didn't. It was a valid point, especially if they wanted us to avoid certain parts of the grounds. Even at this distance, I caught the slight flush on Bevan's cheeks.

"We have two enforcers with us. They will be guiding you to the dorms momentarily," he said. "Now, I'm sure you all have plenty of questions. I'm happy to answer them as we eat and mingle at the welcome supper."

Bevan's voice died out suddenly and he scurried away from the dais. The woman in the enforcer uniform next to me clapped her hands twice for attention. "Girls, follow me."

I waited for most of the others to fall into a loose clump behind her. I slunk along at the back, grateful that no one seemed to be paying me any mind. As we moved through the entrance hall, I made a mental note that the cases were gone. Time to see if Rathbone had kept his word.

I tried to make a mental map of the path from the entrance hall up to the dorms on the second floor. It seemed straightforward enough. Just up the first set of stairs off the hall and straight back.

We reached an archway with several branches and silver placards over them. I spied one bearing the detail N4. It would appear I knew where I was going. The enforcer waved her hands over her head at the signage.

"You'll find your belongings in each room."

People started to manoeuvre around each other, and as I watched them, I realised that they were heading off in groups of three. Only two roommates didn't sound like the worst situation. I traipsed through the arch to N4 and found a washroom off one side and a bedroom with three beds situated against three walls. I didn't see any desk space which begged the question: *where do we study?*

Two of the beds were already taken. I strolled in, trying to act like I belonged—it was my assigned room after all—and checked the case by the third bed. The lock appeared untouched.

"Hi, I'm Eva," one of the girls said.

I turned to look at her. She had the bed against the wall beside me. Dark curls cascaded over her shoulder, accentuating her high cheekbones and mocha-coloured complexion.

"Norah," I answered, and gave her a nod. I glanced at the other girl who sat feverishly going through a textbook. Great, I had to be housed with an overachiever.

"That's Jasmine," Eva offered.

"Jasmine Bourne," she said and set the book aside. "Sorry, I missed your name."

My name caught in my throat. But there was very little chance either of them had any idea about Micah or our connection, right? "Norah Sheehan."

Jasmine's gaze narrowed and she pursed her lips. Something had set her off. "Your brother... He was one of those vandals."

I felt Eva's expectant gaze slide over me before darting back to Jasmine. She didn't seem to know what was going on, but Jasmine clearly had some opinion about Micah. I decided there was no point in denying it—word would be out before long, if it wasn't already.

"He was involved in what happened, but he's been arrested and is waiting for a trial. He's not going to make any more trouble."

Jasmine stood and turned her back to me. I caught the quiver in her body as she began tossing her belongings back into her case. "*He* might not, but that doesn't mean *you* won't."

She didn't even have the decency to look me in the eye when she accused me of whatever the hell she was accusing me of.

"You don't know anything about me. You can't make that sort of assumption," I snapped.

"I know you're a Sheehan. That's all I need to know. I refuse to stay here." Jasmine lugged her case over the threshold, back to the arched entrances to the other girls' dorms.

"You can't just leave," I blurted. Not that I cared if she left. If she judged me just based on my last name, I

43

didn't want her sharing the same space as me.

"Watch me," she spat and stormed out. Her case echoed loudly behind her as she beat a hasty retreat.

I sank onto the bed and looked at Eva, waiting for her to bolt, too. Instead, she crossed her legs, tucking them under her and giving me a bewildered look. "What was that all about?"

"Some people tried to take over the academy last year. One of them was my brother. Apparently sharing his last name is enough to make people assume I'm going to go rogue or whatever." I massaged the bridge of my nose. "I'm not, in case you were wondering."

"Well, I mean, we've not even had any lessons, so how can she expect you to do magic and take over the academy?" Her tone was jovial, if a bit naïve.

I hadn't come here expecting to find anyone to like. But I didn't totally hate Eva.

"Thanks," I muttered and threw myself against the pillows.

I had no desire to go mingle and be social with a bunch of people who probably were in Jasmine's camp rather than Eva's. But my gut told me they paid attention to who didn't show up to group events now more than they used to.

"I know we just met, but can I ask you something?" Eva's voice was hesitant.

"Sure," I sighed.

"Magic comes from your father, right? That's what I was told, anyway."

"Yeah. It's passed from father to child. So, you could have a kid and unless the bloke was unlucky enough to have magic, too, they'd be normal. Why?"

The sound of the shifting mattress was enough to force my eyes open. I watched Eva settle on the end of her bed so she was closer to me.

"I never met my dad. Mum said he skipped out while she was pregnant. But I'm definitely a witch, so he had to be one, too, I guess."

"Shit, sorry. That sucks."

"I'm used to it being just me and Mum. She's one of those tough-as-nails women who fought to make sure I had everything I wanted."

"Sounds brilliant," I said. "I had parents who were so focused on their precious first-born, they forgot about me. And when they did remember I existed, they were constantly disappointed because I was never as good as him."

She propped her chin in her hands. "Well, I know we just met and all, but I'd say you've got something up on him."

I snorted. "Yeah? What's that?"

"You aren't in jail."

I couldn't keep the laughter from escaping. She had a point. I may have to be here, but at least I still technically could do what I wanted within reason. I hadn't seen my brother since his arrest, but I assumed he couldn't even take a piss without someone watching him.

"I needed that," I said, once the laughter faded.

"So, do you think they're going to have decent food at this supper thing?" she said, flipping onto her back.

"I mean, it's academy food, so it's possible it will be decent. Or it could be horrific and we've got no choice but to eat it."

"It's not even day one yet. If they've got anything decent, they'll want to impress us," Eva theorised.

"Probably true," I agreed.

"Would it be awful if we went just long enough to be seen, got food and come back here?"

"Not at all." I watched tension melt out of her shoulders. "I mean, I'm not super social but you seem like you'd fit in fine."

"I get a bit anxious around crowds. Mum thinks it's because I got lost at the shops when I was six. Couldn't find her for like an hour. They had all the workers looking for me."

The fearful look in her eyes drew me in. "How'd you get separated?"

"I don't even remember. Thing is, I just remember

46

thinking I wanted an ice cream, but Mum said we couldn't get any. I guess I really wanted it because they found me at the sweet shop. But, yeah, me and crowds don't really mix."

"Did she at least buy you the ice cream?"

She chuckled. "After telling the shop owner the whole sorry tale, he gave me a cone for free."

"Maybe you had magic then and just didn't know it," I offered with a one-armed shrug.

"Maybe." A pause and then, "Also, if I'm being honest, listening to the other kids talk about magic like it's so commonplace, it makes me uncomfortable. I didn't grow up knowing anything about this world."

"We can dine and dash together," I said.

"Brilliant."

Jasmine may have decided I was evil incarnate just for sharing a last name with my brother, but Eva seemed all right. She at least wanted to get to know me. And if I was going to survive this place, I was going to need someone I could talk to. Having a friend or two wasn't such a bad thing.

Chapter Five

Me and Eva managed to put in an appearance long enough at the welcome supper to be seen, get food and retreat. She hadn't asked me any more questions about my family or my magic the rest of the night and I was relieved to know she wasn't a snorer.

Jasmine never rematerialized, so we both assumed she'd found space in another room. I certainly wasn't going to lose any sleep over her leaving. I'd rather not have to deal with that sort of headache on the daily behind closed doors. Sunday morning dawned and I woke up a full hour before my alarm was set to go off at eight. Groaning, I rolled over to find Eva's bed empty.

A flash of irrational panic lanced through my chest, squeezing out all the air inside. Had she changed her mind and abandoned me, too? I sat up, and as the panic moved from a deafening buzz into a hypersensitive hearing, I picked up the sound of water running in the adjacent washroom. Flopping back against my pillow, I exhaled. The water shut off a few minutes later and my roommate appeared, towel wrapped around her head. She wore stressed denim jeans and a loose sweater. She was no doubt clinging to the last bit of uniqueness before tomorrow stripped us of our individuality. I wasn't looking forward to the uniforms. Most students got to leave all that behind when they went to university. But one of the delights of Braeseth was another three years in a uniform. Joy.

"You okay? You look a little freaked," Eva said as she squeezed the wet from her curls.

"Sorry. I'm fine. Just didn't think you'd be up this early," I mumbled into my shirtsleeve.

"I'm an early riser. Probably ought to have mentioned that yesterday. I didn't mean to wake you."

I waved a hand dismissively. "You didn't. New bed plus new academy jitters did that for me."

"Good. Hey, do you want to go exploring? We don't really have anything we're supposed to do, and I could use someone to stick with."

"Sounds good. Let me just get cleaned up."

She flashed me a grateful grin and set about taming her hair. I unlocked my case and rummaged inside for something to wear. I finally settled on my favourite pair of jogging bottoms and a three-quarter length shirt with a bar of music in varying shades of blue, red, and purple winding across the torso.

"Well, there she is," a high-pitched voice said from our doorway.

I turned to find a girl with the most obvious dye job—no one's hair was that shade of red naturally— standing there blocking my exit and path to the shower. I glanced at Eva, but she just pretended she didn't notice the random girl in our room. Ruby Locks stepped across the threshold uninvited and the sense of unease I'd got from her sudden appearance doubled.

"Can we help you?" I finally asked, crossing my arms over my chest.

She looked around our room, clearly noting the vacant bed. The corners of her mouth turned up at the sight of it. "Celine Wintercrest." She offered a perfectly manicured hand.

I didn't take it. "Why are you in our room?"

"Well, I figured it was time we met. After all, like Dean Bevan said yesterday, we are going to be fast friends." She pointed a finger at Eva. "Get out."

"Excuse me?" Eva's hands stopped moving through her hair.

"You heard me. This doesn't concern you."

I'd known Eva less than a day, but there was no way I'd let this bully talk to her like that. I tossed my clothes back on my bed. "Apologise to her."

"I don't apologise," Celine said coolly.

"Well, you better start now, because no one talks to my friends like that. You barged into our room acting like you own the place. Guess what, you don't."

Celine rolled her eyes at my words and turned so her back was to Eva. "Fine, whatever. She can stay. I just wanted you to know that there are people here who are sympathetic to you and what you've been through." She leaned forward. "One might even say they'd be willing to follow your lead."

The exaggerated wink she dropped at the end of her speech made me want to punch her. Hard. "And what would I be leading?"

"You don't have to be shy about it. I believe in what they started. Someone has to stand up for the underdogs."

There it was. She assumed just because I was Micah's sister, I believed in his stupid cause. "Find yourself another leader. I'm not interested."

She arched a sculpted brow at me and gestured at Eva. "When you're ready for better friends, come find me. I'm in N1. I'm sure we could help you make the transition to a new room, too."

"You might want to get the hell out before I throw you out," I ground out.

Celine gave me a tight-lipped smile and flounced out of the room.

"Bitch," I snarled loud enough for her to hear as she disappeared from view.

"You didn't have to stand up for me," Eva said.

"She's lucky I didn't slug her," I said and scooped up my clothes. "And I meant it. No one treats my friends that way."

She ducked her head, but I caught the glimmer of a smile on her face. "Give me like ten minutes to shower and we can go wander," I added.

I tried to let the warm water wash away the urge to slam my fist into Celine's perfect face. I should have assumed the academy would have its share of popular princesses who thought their shit didn't stink. What I hadn't counted on was them wanting to be friends with me. Not that I could call her offer real friendship. She was looking for a rebellion leader.

"Hey, Norah, did you fall in?" Eva's voice called through the closed door.

I turned the taps to the off position and wrapped the towel around myself. Water dripped down my calves and off the tips of my hair as I opened the door just enough for her to see I wasn't dead. "It's been half an hour," she said.

"Guess I needed a little more me time than I realised."

"It's okay. Take your time."

I dried off and weaved my wet hair into a plait over one shoulder. Somehow, I'd been blessed with hair that dried super quick, so by the time I joined Eva in the corridor, it was dry. Celine's surprise early morning appearance aside, the halls were quiet as we wound our way down to the first floor. The food last night hadn't been half bad and as we reached the entrance hall, my stomach made it known that it needed sustenance.

"Any idea where the canteen is in this place?" I asked.

"They need one of those 'you are here' maps," she answered.

Heavy footsteps approached from behind us, and I spun in time to see a uniformed enforcer approaching, with his ridiculous black-trimmed cloak splayed behind him. It wasn't one of the two who'd been chaperoning us to our dorms. We hadn't stayed long enough at the supper for me to mentally log them all.

"Where are you two headed?" His voice came out in a warm baritone.

"Looking for the canteen," I replied.

The sharp edges of his expression softened slightly, and he waved back the way we'd come. "This way. I thought they gave everyone the tour yesterday."

"Nope," I muttered.

"You aren't wrong about having a map," he added. He'd clearly overheard our conversation. I guess he was trying to endear himself to us—we might be the misfits, but he was out of place here.

I caught Eva's eye and shook my head. She picked up on my meaning as if we'd been communicating nonverbally for ages and we kept our mouths shut as we followed Mr Baritone down a side corridor to a large canteen laid out with dozens of tables. It had a centre buffet with piping hot breakfast foods that set my mouth watering.

"Enjoy," our escort said. "By the way, if you have any questions, or need help, my name is Zachary."

"We'll keep that in mind," I said, and made a beeline for the stacked plates.

"He was totally flirting with you," Eva whispered in my ear as we made our way down the line and piled eggs and sausage and toast onto our plates. I snagged an extra croissant. No one seemed to notice.

"No, he wasn't," I said.

"Trust me. I know flirting when I see it," she said as we found an empty table in a long row of them.

"Then maybe he was flirting with you," I told her, and bit into my toast.

"Mmm, nope. He was all eyes on you."

"Just what I don't want. Maybe Bevan can send out some sort of memo telling everyone to just leave me alone and pretend I'm not even here. I didn't want to come to this dumb academy, anyway."

"You don't seem to like magic," Eva observed.

"It's a bit more complicated than that." I sighed and focused on filling my belly. But Eva had opened up to me last night. It was only fair. "You didn't know your dad, so finding out about magic was a surprise. I've known my whole life that I was supposed to be a witch. Both my parents are, too."

"Didn't you have like a big thing that made it super obvious you had powers?"

"Like a manifestation event?"

"Yeah, I guess that's what they called it. Two years ago, I wasn't in the best place. I was kind of angry about not having a dad. You know, stupid teenage drama wanting to know where I came from."

"What happened?"

"Well, um, it's kind of embarrassing, but I was trying to do research to see what I could find since my mum never really told me much about him. I don't think she knew he had magic. I was searching online, and I posted on some websites and this guy messaged me, said he might have information on my dad."

I didn't like where this was going. The food that I'd shovelled into my stomach was already turning sour at the potential for bad things to happen to my new friend. "He didn't, like, try to do anything hinky to you, did he?"

"Well, he tried to take me for the little money I had but I could tell he was lying."

"How?" The sense of relief that she hadn't been hurt by some creep was tempered by the question of 'what about the magic?'.

"That's the weird thing. I could smell the lies, like he had really bad body odour. Every time he talked, it hit him like a breeze had blown a nasty smell my way."

"So, you can smell when people are lying?" As powers went, it wasn't awful but certainly not flashy.

"I guess. At least that's what I think it is. I went home, talked to Mum, and I got this different smell. It wasn't that she was lying, but she wasn't telling me everything."

"Well, you've got a cooler story than me," I said, and set my utensils down. "I never had anything like that. I had to sit a test to see if I even had magic."

Eva tilted her head to the side. "They have tests for this? I would have taken that over what happened to me."

"Believe me, you wouldn't say that if you'd actually been there. It was a room full of people who looked freaked, like if they were found not to have magic, they'd be disowned. I wouldn't have minded so much if that had been the case."

"But you do have magic, right?"

"They said I had the ability to do it. But I don't think I've ever even accidentally done something small. Anyway, let's talk about something less depressing."

"After this, you want to see if we can find the library? I can't be the only one who noticed there's not really a place to study in the dorms."

"Sure. How about we make it a little more fun, see how many enforcers we can spot?"

"I can't believe people actually managed to curse the building. That's scary."

"Yeah." I didn't say anything else. I knew it had been more than just a curse. But I wasn't in the mood to rehash my brother's wrongdoings.

We finished breakfast and set the dirty plates in a wash bin where a hair-netted woman with thick forearms moved to scoop them up. A few words from her had them sparkling as if they'd never been used. She didn't make eye contact with us before we left.

Wandering the halls proved fruitful. We found one wing full of lecture rooms. At least we had a chance of finding where we had to be tomorrow morning for classes. I also spotted two enforcers posted at each end of the corridor. They were all posted near the toilets on the third floor and by the library, which took up much of the third floor. I took special note that it appeared, at least for today, Zachary's post was outside the lecture rooms.

"You really think he was flirting with me?" I whispered as we left the interior of the complex behind and settled under a tall tree in the courtyard.

"Considering I don't think I heard any of the others even offer up a polite word beyond directing us... If he wasn't flirting, he was definitely being overly friendly."

"Just what I need, to be on their radar, too."

"Not everyone here is going to think you're a ticking time bomb," she said, and nudged my shoulder. "I don't."

"Thanks."

"Also, Celine was totally lying when she said she could get you moved to another room. She doesn't have that authority."

"What do her lies smell like?" I couldn't hide the perverse pleasure of knowing Ruby Locks literally stunk to someone else.

"Bitter oranges. Not the worst smell I've ever come across but the fact that it isn't perfect would probably piss her off."

"You noticed that god awful dye job, too, right?" I snickered.

"It was like she dumped an entire vat of hot sauce on her head," she giggled.

I might have been forced to be here to learn to harness whatever meagre magic I possessed, but at least I had one person I could count on to be in my corner. As much as I was dreading the lessons to come, I tried to tend the tiny ember of hope that with Eva by my side, I'd be able to survive this place relatively unscathed.

Chapter Six

Monday morning arrived bright and noisy as everyone rushed around, hoping to not be *that* person late on their first day. Someone had come through and posted a timetable for the week of lessons. First up was energy manipulation at nine o'clock. Me and Eva were both up and in the canteen by eight.

"Bet most of them are scrambling to figure out where to go," I said, trying not to sound too smug as I sipped my latte. I'd been so focused on food yesterday that I'd missed the large selection of hot drinks.

"What do you think energy manipulation is going to be like? I kind of assumed we'd be focusing on whatever it is we can do."

I shrugged a shoulder. "I guess since not everyone has a specific power, they've got the teach us the basics."

"I hope the instructor is chill. I figure a class all about energy could get dangerous fast."

"They want us to learn. I doubt they're going to let anything happen that could put us in mortal peril. At least not on day one. Save that for day two."

"I just wish we didn't have to have it with the whole first year. I was enjoying not having to see Celine all day yesterday," Eva murmured.

"Same."

By quarter to nine, we'd headed for the class corridor. I spied Zachary at the far end of the hall. He gave me a nod when he spotted me. I was starting to think Eva was right. Maybe he did like me.

"The timetable didn't list a room number," Eva whispered in my ear as we stood in the centre of the corridor.

I was positioned in such a way that I could still see Zachary at the far end. He held up a hand and flashed four fingers and gestured to his left. "Uh, let's try the fourth room," I said, and dragged my roommate lightly by the wrist.

The door was unlocked, and we were the first ones in the lecture room. Thankfully, someone had scrawled Energy Manipulation on the board at the front of the room.

"How'd you know that?"

I settled into a desk in the back of the room. "My stalker gave me a heads up."

"So, you are accepting that he's interested in you," she said, and sat beside me.

"I wouldn't go that far, but he was definitely helping me out."

Eva let out a soft hiccup of laughter and pulled out a notepad and pen. I did the same and leaned back, waiting for the class to begin. Slowly, as the clock ticked closer to the top of the hour, the rest of our classmates funnelled in.

"They're all staring at me," I hissed under my breath as the tenth person looked at me and made sure there were at least two rows of seats between them and me.

"There are just a lot of seats to pick from," Eva offered feebly.

Celine waltzed in followed by a gaggle of girls. Her gaze slid over to our corner and she led her entourage to the seats two in front of us. Great. She didn't have a problem sitting near us. I spotted Jasmine walk in and look at the smattering of empty seats. There weren't that many except the ones near me and Eva.

Jasmine approached a guy with a mop of messy sandy hair on the far side of the room. "You're in my seat."

He looked up at her. "Don't see your name on it."

"Well, it is. Now, move."

"Why should I?" he demanded.

She thrust a hand in my direction. "I'm not sitting near that."

"Take your seats please," a familiar bass voice called as Instructor Rathbone walked into the lecture room.

Clearly not dumb enough to make a bad name for herself on day one, Jasmine slunk into the furthest open seat from me, which put her right in front of Rathbone's desk. Something told me Jasmine wasn't overly put out about being in his line of sight.

Rathbone shoved his hands into the pockets of his uniform trousers. Even the instructors here were forced to wear something similar to our clothes. *Cult, much?* I noticed today he wore his long hair in a low man bun at the nape of his neck.

I watched as he turned slowly from one side of the lecture room to the other. "Good, looks like everyone managed to find their way here. Have to say, that's quite the rarity with most first years."

"They didn't put the room number on the timetable," Jasmine complained loudly.

"Clearly an oversight," Rathbone said. The twinkle in his eye suggested otherwise.

Jasmine's pout was audible as she slumped back against her chair. I leaned closer to Eva. "God, she's wound tight."

"Be grateful you missed the battle over the beds. She insisted she had to have the one closest to the door. If she'd stayed, I wouldn't have been surprised if she'd drawn lines on the floor and flipped out if we crossed into her space."

Rathbone tapped the board with his knuckles, making a loud enough thump to draw my attention.

"So, energy manipulation," he began, just as Celine's hand shot up into the air. I was surprised she didn't fly out of her seat with how forcefully she'd thrust it above her head.

"Yes."

"Aren't we going to go around and introduce everyone?"

"I'm pretty sure that's what yesterday's festivities were meant for. You'll have time to get to know each other outside of lessons. My job is to make sure you learn the fundamentals of this discipline."

"Oh." She sighed and lowered her hand.

"Okay, he's definitely the coolest instructor here," I stage-whispered.

Eva hid a snicker behind her hand as Rathbone stepped out from behind his desk.

"So, I'm sure many of you are expecting to learn how to form and throw energy balls."

Some of the guys on the other side of the room started elbowing each other and leaning forward in their seats. Rathbone held up a hand to temper their enthusiasm. "Well, you'll get a chance to try once you can routinely handle the building blocks that get you there."

He held up both of his hands and tiny blue sparking lightning bolts jumped between his thumbs and forefingers. "Conjuring a spark this size is the first step, and what we're going to be working on today."

Jasmine turned and stared straight at me. "Oh, that's

easy."

"Well, it sounds like we've got a volunteer to demonstrate," Rathbone said and ushered Jasmine to stand beside him.

I leaned forward, propped my elbows on the desk, and rested my chin in my hands. I gave her my full attention. She thought she was better than me? Fine. I would do what I could to make her feel uncomfortable as hell.

"Whenever you're ready," Rathbone said.

Jasmine wet her lips and rubbed her hands on the front of her trousers. To the casual observer, it looked like nerves. I suspected she was trying to build up some static electricity. She had no clue what she was doing. Jasmine held up her right hand and the very faint flicker of a charge danced from the pad of her thumb to her forefinger.

"I can do better," she huffed, and her brow furrowed.

Her jaw set as she gritted her teeth, and the spark grew and leapt back and forth until it was a steady current. She fixed me with a haughty expression. "See."

Rathbone cleared his throat and gestured to her vacant seat. "Thank you."

He settled against the front edge of his desk, looking relaxed.

"Magic is fuelled by emotion. You have to want it to

happen. But be intentional with that desire. Channel your focus into the desire to take the energy that exists all around us and make it obey your command. Now, before you all get too excited, this takes time and practice. I don't expect most of you to be successful today."

That statement only made Jasmine even smugger. She kept crackling little bolts between her hands for the next ten minutes as Rathbone moved through the rows of desks, letting us watch him as he summoned the energy and let it dance along his skin.

Across the room, one of the other girls let out a squeal as the electricity zipped from her thumb back up over her hand, igniting the tiny hairs along her arm. Rathbone swooped in, patting them out with the hem of his shirtsleeve. He spent a good two minutes examining her arm to make sure she didn't need medical attention. Satisfied she would be okay and offering a "Good effort. Make sure you focus on keeping it just between your fingers for now," he moved on.

He stopped near me and did his little show and tell for the millionth time. I hadn't bothered to try it yet. What was the point if I wasn't going to succeed, anyway? And if I did, it would only fuel the hatred from my classmates. No doubt they'd be whispering 'She can do it because she's got bad intentions and wants to rule the world.' Eva sat beside me, brow furrowed in concentration as she tried to make it happen. All she succeeded in doing was statically charging her mess of curls, so they stood up at wild angles. When Rathbone arrived, she was busy patting them down with her palms.

"How's it going over here?" Rathbone said and turned his attention to me and Eva. Celine and her cronies turned in their chairs to watch, too.

"No luck yet," I said with a noncommittal shrug.

"It usually helps to try," he replied.

"I have," I said weakly.

"Let's not start the semester off with lies, Norah," he said softly.

The way he used my name, when he hadn't bothered to address anyone else that way, gave me mixed feelings. He clearly remembered me from two days ago, which was sort of flattering, but it also meant he was paying particular attention to me. Like he had some other reason for keeping a close eye on me. Which was definitely *not* flattering.

"I think I managed it, Instructor Rathbone," Celine interjected and waved her hand in his face. A tiny flicker of bluish-purple light danced along her fingertips. It fizzled out, and she pulled her hand away from his face.

"Keep practicing, then," Rathbone said, without taking his eyes off me.

The lack of attention on her clearly annoyed the hell

66

out of Celine, but she turned away and her groupies did the same. If only Jasmine would stop staring at me from the front of the room. Her voice carried clearly.

"Guess she's not as powerful as everyone said."

Anger flashed through me, igniting the nerves in my hands. I might not be able to conjure lightning on the outside but it sure as hell felt like I was doing it on the inside. I tried to visualise what I'd seen Rathbone and Jasmine do. I just wanted there to be a single bolt of energy, just to prove a belonged here. Just once. Nothing happened, other than my frustration doubling. I balled my hands into fists. "See, guess I'm just shit at this."

"Practise. With time and discipline, everyone in this room will be able to manipulate the energy around them." He looked at me. "Remember, emotion drives your magic. But just because you've got a strong emotion doesn't mean it's going to make things work how you expect."

He stepped back and addressed the class as a whole.

"Your assignment for our next class is to practise. That should be enough time to make good progress toward being able to sustain a bolt for at least thirty seconds."

The cacophony of voices and shuffling feet in the corridor signalled that it was time to switch lessons. I wasn't in the mood to go learn more useless knowledge for things I had no hope of doing.

"Looks like we've got botany next," Eva said, and nudged my shoulder.

"Yeah, I'll be there in a minute," I said, taking my time to pack up my notebook and bag.

"I'll save you a seat," Eva said, and wound past Celine and her admirers. I loitered as the rest of the class filtered out until it was just me and Rathbone.

I realised he probably had another class to teach and slung my bag over my shoulder.

"Thanks," I offered when I reached his desk.

"For?" he prompted.

"For making sure my case got to my room like you said. I appreciate it."

"I know you don't think you deserve to be here, but that doesn't mean you shouldn't try to learn what we're teaching. You might surprise yourself. I know it's within you."

"What, are you like a mind reader or something?" The question was out of my mouth before I thought better of it. I wasn't used to watching my mouth, on account of no-one ever noticing me before.

Rathbone laughed. "Believe me, I wouldn't be working in an academy if I could pry into personal thoughts. I was a teenager once. I don't need the constant reminder of just how much time teenagers spend thinking about sex."

"Yeah, I guess that would kind of be a rubbish power."

"I can see that you're reluctant to try to control your magic. No extra special skill. Just observation," he said in a reassuring tone.

"I think you might be giving me too much credit. I had to sit a test to even get in."

"You and a decent portion of the other students in your year. And every year before and after you, too."

"I appreciate you trying to help, but you'd be better off focusing on someone like Jasmine. She's clearly got skill and wants to use it."

"Every student deserves my attention, whether they think they're worthy or not. And remember, the stronger the emotion, the more powerful the magic. But that's not always a good thing. Part of what we're trying to teach you is how to harness the right levels of power for the spells you're trying to cast."

I waved a hand toward the door. "Right, well, I better get going. Don't want to be late for my next lesson."

"Promise me you're going to practise. Not everyone is meant to be amazing at every skill, but you won't know what you're good at until you give it a go."

"I'll try," I said, and for a moment, even meant it.

He gave me a satisfied smile, and I headed out the

door, spotting Eva waiting for me outside a lecture room at the far end of the corridor.

The first lesson had been a bust and despite my promise to Rathbone, I still didn't want to be here. I couldn't use whatever power existed inside me. Everyone would have been better off if I'd had my magic bound like I'd wanted. Then I wouldn't be stuck in this place where most of the people hated me on principle or wanted me to lead some stupid revolution. There was no chance that this experience was going to get any better. My fleeting hope that I might fit in after finding a friend in Eva was just a childish fantasy. Magic was real, but it sure as hell wasn't fair. Not when it came to me.

Chapter Seven

By Wednesday, I was convinced that all of these classes were going to be utter hell. All around me, my classmates were starting to show signs of picking up on the easier spells, and I just couldn't get it. Not that I was trying very hard, admittedly. I was lounging in the library, staring out the window, when Eva stuck her head around the shelves.

"You coming?" she whispered. Clearly, she didn't want to get on the librarian's bad side. Probably for the best—this place was pretty much my one refuge, and I didn't much fancy getting kicked out.

I turned to look at my roommate and my brow scrunched together as I tried to recall what class it was. "Nah, I'm not in this one," I muttered when it hit me that we were scheduled for unique magics lessons now.

"You could, I dunno, audit it or something, right? Learn the theory?" She pressed. "Come on, Nor, I don't want to go to this one by myself."

I shook my head.

"Sorry, Eva, it doesn't work that way. Only students with unique magics can go to that class." A small lance of guilt ran through me that I was relieved I had an excuse not to find one more class to fail in.

"You'll be fine," I promised her. "I'm going to try to study. I told Rathbone I'd actually try to do that whole energy thing. I mean, I may be rubbish at all this magic stuff, but if stupid Jasmine could do it, then I should be able to."

Eva pouted as she shifted her bag to her other shoulder. "Fine. I'll find you before lunch."

I was halfway out of my seat, the words 'I'm sorry' hanging unspoken on my lips by the time she disappeared. I wouldn't call what just happened a fight. Going to class wasn't worth that sort of emotional investment—but I'd definitely disappointed her. I knew she was still nervous around the other students, especially since she hadn't grown up with magic. But she had loads more magical talent and ability than me. She belonged in the unique magics class.

I turned back to the window, but the serenity that had begun to settle over me before her interruption vanished. Annoyance took its place. The soft hazy clouds outside, floating through a calming blue sky, only irritated me more. Pity was never a feeling I enjoyed, especially when it was directed inward. Feeling sorry for yourself never got you anywhere in life. *'You're not alone.'* Kelsey's voice echoed in the back of my head.

I might not be able to moan to Eva right this second—and I likely had some grovelling to do when we ate lunch—but she wasn't the only friend I had. Well, okay, friend might have been a stretch, but there was someone else who'd offered to be a sounding board and a kind ear. I slammed the books in front of me closed and shoved them back in my bag. I was pretty sure the studying wasn't helping, anyway. The communication stone Kelsey had given me was stashed in the bottom of my case. The way she'd handled it in the Circle's headquarters suggested it wasn't something everyone had access to.

The corridors were eerily quiet as I made my way toward the girls' dormitories. I tried not to let the silence press in against me. Everyone else was in class. That was the reason my footsteps echoed painfully in my ears with every step. I took the stairs to the second floor two at a time. I tried to plan out what I would say if Kelsey answered my call. After all, it had been a few weeks since we'd talked, and I had no idea if she really meant she wanted me to stay in touch. Maybe she was relieved I hadn't contacted her.

I shouldered the door to the second floor open and slammed into a meaty form. Staggering back, I barely caught myself, narrowly avoiding falling on my backside. I blinked up to find Zachary standing in front of me. He held out a hand to me.

"You aren't, like, following me, are you?" I blurted.

"Nope," he answered.

"Good. Could give a girl ideas otherwise," I said in as

light a tone as I could muster and tried to sidestep him, but he moved to block my path.

"You need to find another way," he said, crossing his arms over his chest.

"Yeah, not really going to work. See, you all are very particular about where we go, and this is the only way I know to get to the dorms."

"You should be in class," he commented.

"Right. Well, see, I forgot something very important," I lied. "Can't do the lesson without it, and it happens to be in my dorm. So, if you could just move for like twenty seconds, I'll be out of your hair. You won't even notice I was in there."

He shook his head. "Can't do it."

"Seriously? Come on. I didn't know we had dictators running this place."

He didn't react to my insult, which was annoying on a whole other level. What good was having an enforcer flirting with me if I couldn't use it to bend the rules? Wasn't that the whole reason people got in good with people in power? To skirt the rules that were just plain stupid.

"You need to find another way or go back to class. This area is off limits right now," Zachary replied, his tone harsh and his eyes cold.

"This wasn't even the part of the grounds that got hit

with the curse," I complained.

Zachary just stood there like a statue. The longer he went without speaking, the more I began panicking that they'd found the communication stone. I didn't think Kelsey would set me up, but she knew I wasn't a fan of the druids in general and the Circle in particular. And the way Celine spoke, they had good reason to worry that the sentiments expressed by my brother and the people he was involved with hadn't been wiped out. They were just looking in the wrong place. And I was so, so sick of everyone assuming I was the guilty one here.

"I thought you and I had an understanding," I snapped.

The corners of his mouth twitched, like he wanted to speak but he wasn't going to risk his job or whatever they were doing by spilling details to me. I flipped him off for good measure before I started down the stairs.

"Those enforcers can be such arrogant arseholes, can't they?" Celine's voice filled the stairwell.

"Don't know what you're talking about," I said, coming to stand on the landing in between the treads.

She fixed me with a sugary smile. "It's hard not to eavesdrop when you were practically shouting at him."

"I wasn't shouting," I snapped.

"Well, your voices carried. A lot."

I rolled my eyes and shouldered past her to the first-floor corridor. I wasn't sure where I planned to go, but it involved being as far from Celine as possible. Unfortunately, she obviously didn't get the message because she fell into step with me. Like we were friends.

"Shouldn't you be in class?" I said.

"Funny, I could say the same to you."

"I don't have a unique power so no reason to go to that class. What's your excuse?" Not that I cared.

She flipped her obnoxiously bright red hair over one shoulder. "I'm ditching. I manifested super young, so I've been practicing my powers for years. There isn't much these losers can teach me, anyway."

"You know that's illegal, right? Practicing magic away from the academy before you're qualified or whatever?" She just shrugged in reply, like the laws didn't apply to her. Maybe she thought they didn't. I gritted my teeth, hating myself for wanting to ask her more questions. "If you hate it here, why come?"

She looked at me like I'd lost it. "Because I don't want to be bound, of course."

"Bound?"

"You do know what being bound means?" She arched a brow, giving me a condescending look that made me want to whack her.

"Yes I know what being—" I broke off, and started again. "You mean, if I hadn't shown up here, they'd have bound my magic?"

She nodded. Shit. It would have saved me a whole lot of trouble if anyone had told me that. I wondered if I could still get rid of my magic by dropping out...only I wasn't exactly sure how to do that.

"Anyway," she said, tossing her mane of hair, "my family on both sides has graduated from Braeseth going back to my three times great grandparents. It's a legacy thing."

"Guess you didn't want to be the one to stand out from the crowd, huh?"

She scoffed. "Oh, there are plenty of ways to do that, once I have full control of my magic."

I didn't like where this conversation was going. "Well, good luck with that whole standing out thing."

I turned down the corridor leading to the canteen. Maybe I could sneak in early and grab Eva an apology tin of biscuits. They actually made halfway decent chocolate ones that she'd raved over all week.

"I know you think you don't have a place here," Celine called after me, "but you do."

It was enough to stop me in my tracks. I whirled round to face her. "You get that I'm not him, don't you?"

"Families are funny like that," she said, a cold smile playing across her lips. "They shape us more than we want to admit. Sometimes in ways we don't even realise until we're standing there finding our voice for the first time."

"I don't want a part in whatever you're concocting." I'd meant the words to come out angry, but instead, they sounded like I was trying to convince myself as much as I was trying to convince her, and I didn't like the hollow ring to them. I shook my head. I wasn't about to become besties with someone like her; someone who thought it was okay to treat people like Eva like dirt because they weren't of any use to her.

"Academies are great for all sorts of learning," Celine said. The glint in her eyes and the way she bared her teeth reminded me of a predator preparing to take down prey. "You'll learn that I don't give up easily."

"You're gonna be disappointed then," I said, and stormed off down the hall to the canteen.

* * *

Loitering outside the unique magics lecture room, I tried to stay out of the flow of people spilling out while still making sure Eva saw me waiting. She didn't speak, but did fall into step with me. I kept walking toward the front of the building.

"Aren't we getting lunch?" She sounded worn out. I'd always heard that using magic was draining, not that I'd had any experience of it myself, of course.

I patted my bag. "I had a little time to kill so I may

have nicked some sandwiches ahead of everyone else. They even wrapped them to stay warm. Those kitchen mages might be the one good thing about this place, you know."

A bit of the weariness lifted from her face and she flashed a small smile. We headed for the spot we'd claimed as ours beneath a towering tree. Someone had thought to put a table and bench there but no one else seemed inclined to sit there. At least none of the older students had tried to claim it. Maybe my pariah bubble extended beyond just our year. Good to be wanted.

"Biscuits!" Eva exclaimed as I passed her the tin.

"I'm sorry I was so bitchy earlier," I said, and took a bite of my food.

"You must not have had a lot of proper rows because if you thought that was a fight worth bribing me with chocolate biscuits, you're going to be sorry when it's something big," she replied with a grin.

"I know it wasn't a row. I just, I know you don't like having to spend time with the lot of them. Crowds and all."

"It wasn't so terrible. Didn't have to deal with stuck-up Celine."

"That's because she was stalking me."

"What?"

"After you left, I decided I was going to go back to

the dorm. Not ideal for studying but I just didn't want to be sitting alone in such an open space like a loser. The enforcers had blocked the entry."

"They can't do that, can they?"

"Well, they did. I don't know what was really going on."

"Maybe Bevan will make an announcement. Maybe they've almost finished clearing up the curse."

I shook my head. "I never believed that bullshit explanation. They're clearly scared of something. I bet they were looking for something."

"Like what?"

I shrugged and helped myself to one of her biscuits. "Dunno. But they clearly don't trust any of us."

"They're instructors. They're here to teach and protect us. Not hurt us," Eva argued.

"Maybe." Aside from Rathbone, none of the instructors had given me the warm and fuzzies. And I wouldn't call him a teddy bear. More like a bear trying to keep his unruly cubs in line.

"So, why was Celine following you?"

"Damned if I know," I answered, and stretched out against the trunk of the tree.

"She does seem fascinated with you," Eva said, rolling her sandwich wrapper into a tiny ball.

"Not the word I'd use. More like she's obsessed with

my brother and expects me to be just like him."

"Isn't that a normal feeling for people with siblings? You feel like you should be like them?" she probed.

"I don't know. I mean, I tried to be like him, to be just as good as him and it bit me in the arse because I'm nowhere near as skilled as he is. I've decided to say the hell with it and be my own person. I don't have a choice about being here. So, if I can just stay under the radar, that's all I want."

"I'm going to sound like a broken record, and the rest of the class may want to keep their distance, but I'm not going anywhere. And not just because I don't want to room with any of the rest of the girls in our year."

I snorted. "I wouldn't either."

"You treated me like I belonged, even when you didn't have to. Hell, we still don't know each other that well and you're bribing me with sweets. That is the mark of a true friend."

I couldn't help smiling at her words. "I didn't come here expecting to find someone who got me. I guess there's some small force in the universe who isn't on the 'let's screw Norah' bandwagon. You're probably my first proper friend in ages. So, thank you."

Her smile widened, and she held the crumpled wrapper out to me. "Want to see if you can make electricity jump from this? I mean, it's a conductive material anyway, right?"

"Isn't that cheating?"

"Think of it more like…an extra boost."

I shrugged. I hadn't been able to make anything happen when I'd tried in class. Or the couple of times I'd half-arsed it late at night, staring at the ceiling in our dorm. But I wasn't going to get any better if I didn't make a real effort. I just wasn't sure I wanted to try, when Celine's words about being bound were still ringing in my ears. But this was Eva, and even though I hadn't known her for long, I really didn't want to fall out with her. I watched as she rubbed the wrapper on her knee to pick up an electric charge.

I focused on my left hand, trying to block out the rest of the world around me. I could hear the faint crackle of the pent-up energy wanting release. I stretched out my fingers, urging the power to jump from the wrapper into my hand. A nagging doubt crept in, reminding me I'd never controlled my magic, not like Micah, but I shoved it down. I latched onto Eva's friendship, and her belief that I was worth it. The spark, a pale blue blip, flickered off the wrapper and settled on the tip of my pointer finger.

"Oh, shit," I said as the charged slid down my finger to bounce to my thumb and back again.

"You just needed the right jumping off point," Eva said.

Well, damn. That nugget of hope was infectious, and we fell into fits of laughter, leaning against one another as the spark twinkled and buzzed against my skin. Maybe I wasn't as terrible at this whole magic thing as I assumed.

Chapter Eight

Dean Bevan never did make any sort of statement about why the dorms had been off limits. By the time classes were over, we'd been able to get back in with no questions asked. A quick survey of my belongings had confirmed they'd been rifled through—someone had tried to fold my clothes back—but nothing appeared missing. Since then, I'd taken to carrying the communication stone in my bag. I didn't know if it was what they were after, but I didn't want to take any chances.

The days and weeks crept past, and September became October, and a rare dry Saturday found me and Eva out in the grounds.

"Can you believe it's almost been a month since we started classes?" Eva mused as we sat on the academy's front steps. Neither of us had fancied wading out to our usual spot after yesterday's rain, sacrificing its seclusion—we were never disturbed there, either by the other students, or the druids, who showed no sign of finishing their working and leaving—in favour of dry feet.

I watched the other students wandering around the grounds in their weekend clothes. I had to admit I relished those two days out of uniform.

"It doesn't feel quite real," I said.

She held up her right hand, and branches of electricity lanced from her thumb and across each finger. We still weren't to the point of making full-on energy balls. I didn't think Rathbone wanted to get there any earlier than necessary. We couldn't do a ton of damage with just little bolts of electricity.

I turned my focus to my own hand. I was getting better at conjuring the electricity without needing a starter aid. I'd even earned Rathbone's praise in class last week for the progress I was making.

"You are definitely getting better," Eva said with an affectionate shoulder nudge that almost made me electrocute her. Not that she'd have felt much—my magic still lacked any real power. I rolled my eyes.

"I can keep it going for a whole ten seconds now. Meanwhile, you're going to be shooting lightning bolts out of your hands like freaking Zeus before Halloween."

"Everyone learns at their own pace."

"And some people are just naturals at this stuff. Like you," I reminded her.

She opened her mouth to disagree, then caught the look on my face and snapped it shut again. We both knew she wasn't going to win that argument any time soon. I didn't mind—it wasn't like I'd come here expecting to set the world on fire...or electrocute it. I propped myself up on my elbows and closed my eyes, enjoying the autumn air on my face. It made a nice change from being cooped up inside the academy—either by the instructors, or the British weather.

"Uh oh, enforcer alert." Eva's tone was a mix of amusement and anxiety.

I opened my eyes and caught sight of Zachary standing at the foot of the stairs. I gestured for him to go around—I wasn't in the mood to move for him—but he had something in his hands, and held it out to me.

"You've got a letter," he said and offered the envelope to me.

"So, they've got you delivering mail now? Whose arse did you forget to kiss this week?" I replied.

A bemused smile tugged at his lips as he thrust the envelope into my lap.

"It looks pretty official. Might want to open it before too long." He stepped back. "And who says I have to kiss anyone's arse?"

I made a show of trying to peer at his backside. "Well, I don't see any lipstick marks on yours."

"The key to a good arse-kissing is to hide the evidence."

I rolled my eyes, and he melted into a group of students heading off grounds. Eva waited a solid ten seconds before punching me in the arm. "He's totally into you. And you are definitely into him."

"I am not into him," I protested. "He's annoying as hell."

"Right, because you weren't just checking out his backside."

"I wasn't!" I was *not* into him. I held up the envelope he'd delivered. "Oh, look, a distraction."

"Nice segue, Nor," she snickered.

I slipped my finger under the flap of the envelope and pulled out the single sheet of paper. I scanned it once, and then a second time. The words printed on it took far longer than they should have to sink in. I blinked once, twice, but the text remained unchanged.

"Are you okay?" Her words sounded so far away.

"Halloween," I murmured.

"What about it?"

In my peripheral vision I caught her hands flexing. She was resisting the urge to pull the paper from my hands.

"My brother's trial is happening on Halloween."

"Oh. Well, you knew it would happen eventually."

"I didn't think it would be this soon." I pushed myself to my feet and folded the paper and stuffed it back inside. I supposed it was for the best. They couldn't keep him in limbo forever. Best to get it over with.

"Where are you going?" She was on her feet right after me.

"I need to see Dean Bevan. I need to be there."

She hesitated, a flicker of confusion passing through her eyes.

"You aren't what I'd call your brother's biggest fan."

"He's still my brother. Whatever he did, whatever happens, he deserves to have a familiar face there."

"I'll come, too," she offered, but I shook my head.

"No. This is something I need to do myself. I'll meet you back in the dorm. We can do that magical law essay."

"I'll be waiting," she said, giving me a sympathetic look before she retreated back inside.

We parted ways in the entryway, and I turned to the left. Dean Bevan's office was located off the lecture hall where he'd greeted us on day one. I'd never had a reason to set foot in there. I didn't know if he was even around—but I didn't know where else to look for him, either.

Unlike the Circle, he didn't have a gatekeeper to stop students from bothering him. His door was open, and he sat at a low desk, pouring over a newspaper. My feet sunk into the thick carpeting, and I was immediately annoyed that it muffled my entrance.

"Excuse me, sir," I said, as loud as I dared, though my voice still came out hushed and raspy.

He looked up and blinked. After a split second, recognition dawned on his face and he set the paper aside. "Ms Sheehan, isn't it?"

"Uh, yeah. I got this letter about…well, about my brother's trial. It's happening on Halloween. I know he's the last person you probably want to think about but—"

He raised a hand and cut me off before I could ramble any more.

"You have permission to attend."

"I…I do?"

"Yes. I'll excuse you from classes for the day and arrange for transportation to and from the Circle for you."

"That's really nice of you." I tried and failed to keep the cynicism from my tone. I'd expected him to fight me on this, or maybe call in a couple of druids to interrogate me about why I wanted to be there. Bevan exhaled heavily and leaned back in his chair.

"I suspect there are many people treating you like you are your brother. I do not see that." He cleared his throat and raised an eyebrow at me. "Now, unless you have anything else, I believe you have a weekend to enjoy— before you return to applying yourself to your studies."

I nodded mutely and retraced my steps back to the entryway. I knew I should be relieved that getting permission to go to the trial hadn't been a fight, but the sceptic in me was already wondering what motive he might have for letting me go. I'd no doubt have an enforcer escort to keep tabs on me. Did he want me to see justice meted out as some form of deterrent? He'd just said he didn't believe Micah and I were at all alike, so that didn't seem likely, but I couldn't know for certain. It wasn't like I was the one with the ability to sniff out lies. As I retreated to the dorms, I momentarily considered asking Bevan if I could pick my escort.

'You so fancy Zachary,' Eva's voice taunted in my head.

"Oh, sod off," I muttered aloud as I headed upstairs.

I stepped into the room and the scent of cinnamon wafted from the bed we'd been using to stash mix of dirty plates on, and clothes underneath. Somehow, we'd lucked into not getting a third roommate forced on us. Or maybe there'd just been no volunteers to take Jasmine's place. Either way, I wasn't complaining.

"You looked like you needed a pick-me-up," Eva said, and presented me with cinnamon cakes drizzled with sugary topping and a tall glass of latte.

"Thanks," I said and snatched a cake, shoving it into my mouth.

"So, what did Bevan say? Can you go?" She peered at me over the top of her magical law textbook.

"Yep. No fight, even. He's ensuring I've got someone to get me there and back," I answered once I'd swallowed. I caught the mischievous look in her eye and cut it off at the pass. "And no, I don't get to pick who chaperones me."

Well, probably didn't. It was best not to encourage her.

"Fine." She let the book fall into her lap so she could wave a balled-up pair of white socks. "I surrender."

I pulled out my own textbook and flipped to the chapter on punishments. A fitting topic given what was looming in less than a month's time. "So, what are we supposed to be writing about again?"

"You would be so lost without me," Eva sighed. "We have to discuss whether we believe the punishment system is ethical or not."

"Right. Because a bunch of teenagers who can't make good decisions about who to shag should be giving their opinions on laws," I grumbled.

"I'll have you know I'm quite a good judge. I made the very sound decision to avoid sleeping with anyone in this place."

"That's because you're not stupid."

"I also happen to think most of the punishments are pretty barbaric. I mean, I've never been for killing people. How does that really help?"

"I agree with you there. There's too much death in the world as is. Why contribute to it? I'm glad we don't have the death punishment. I never understood why the shifters use it."

"I don't get why they don't use more alternative methods—like memory modification, that sort of thing. For smaller crimes, anyway. People aren't born evil or wanting to be criminals. I have to believe a lot of it is circumstantial."

"I don't know, some people would be safer if they didn't have magic. So, I don't think they should get rid of binding people when they've done something really bad. Murdered people or whatever. Do that and lock them up. That seems reasonable."

Eva shook her head. "I don't even see that as a reasonable method. I mean magic is as much a part of someone as their hair or eye colour, right? That's how it was explained to me, anyway."

"It's genetic. Yeah. So?"

"So, you're basically cutting off people from a part of themselves that exists. It's like if you decided to punish people by cutting off their hands."

I shrugged. "They used to do that."

"Okay, bad example, but you get my point, right? You're depriving people of a part of who they are. I may not have known about my magic for a long time but the moment I found out, it felt like a piece of me that I'd been missing was put into place." Her mouth hung open like she wanted to say something else. "I just think that the system is antiquated and should be updated."

"I tried to do it," I said, tossing the book aside.

"Do what?"

"Have my magic bound. Before I came here. Before I knew that not attending meant I'd be bound, anyway. I petitioned the Circle, but they said no."

"You were willing to give up a piece of your identity?"

"I don't see it like you do, Eva. For me, it's this reminder of how I've failed. You've seen me. I'm just not good at magic. I never used it before coming here, so how could I miss what I didn't have?"

She stared at me, her lips moving silently as if trying to work through her response in a way that wouldn't offend me. "They obviously said no."

"Twice. I went there a few weeks before classes started to beg them to do it, but they refused. Insisted I had to come here to learn to control what power I did have."

"I'm glad they made you come here. I don't think I could have survived so far without you."

"I'm sure you would have found someone else to hang out with."

She pointed to the closed door to the room. "Have you missed that no one talks to me?"

"They would, if you weren't seen with me."

"Maybe, but I am still glad you came and didn't have your magic bound. You aren't a criminal. You didn't do anything wrong that would warrant them taking away a piece of you."

I wasn't sure I was going to agree with her on her perspective on totally revamping the criminal justice system in our world—some people were just too dangerous to be allowed access to that sort of power—but I could appreciate that my friend was glad we'd met. And I suspected she was going to write a killer essay on the topic. I could pull something together. I definitely agreed that the death sentence should never come back into our justice system. Lock people up where they wouldn't hurt anyone but themselves, sure. And find a way to keep them from using their powers to escape. I wasn't ready to try to rehabilitate every criminal locked away. Some people didn't deserve freedom or leniency. As I sat there, a knot of discomfort settled in the pit of my stomach. I realised I was so conditioned to accept the level of power the druids held over all of us, I hadn't even bothered to think that the system should change.

"I suppose it hasn't been all bad, having to learn to use my powers. I mean, you are definitely the highlight of the last month of my life. And I guess it's been kind of fun learning to make little baby lightning bolts."

"You are getting so much better," Eva said, pouncing on the change of direction our conversation had taken. "You don't even need a boost anymore. And Rathbone totally sees your progress."

"Too bad he's the only one." The small smiles he offered did make our lessons a little less unbearable.

"Hey, at least you haven't accidentally killed any of your plants in botany. I had to ask Instructor Weaver for new ones last week because I overwatered mine and they wilted. I'm not entirely sure she understood what I was asking at first. Then, when I pointed to my pots, she sort of glared at me, muttered something about inattentive children and walked off."

I laughed at the image of Eva having to go beg Weaver for more plants. The woman looked like she belonged in some sort of home for the elderly. She shouted at us—probably because she couldn't hear—and squinted through thick-lensed cats-eyeglasses. It was a wonder she kept anything alive, either. I suspected that given everything that happened last year, new staff were hard to come by and the ones they managed to keep hold of were the ones who wouldn't be scared off by some student uprising. Maybe I owed Weaver more respect.

"Well, if you ever need someone to electrocute your succulents, I'm your girl," I said, bouncing the little lightening bolt between my thumb and forefinger.

Eva chuckled and turned back to crafting her essay. I tried to focus on mine, but the thought of Micah's impending trial consumed me. What sort of punishment would they pass on him? He deserved some sort of repercussions for his actions, but what? The thought of Eva's rehabilitation methods didn't sound so bad when I pictured my brother's face as he sat locked in a cell, all alone. He'd never done well being by himself. That might have been part of his problem. Squeezing my eyes shut to banish the image, I settled into the assignment. I'd have plenty of time to stress over my brother's fate once the work was done.

Chapter Nine

Somehow, October vanished before my eyes. One minute I was lamenting the stupidity of botany with Eva, and the next I rolled over to see October 31st on the calendar. I hadn't said anything else about Micah's trial since getting the notice about it. I hadn't wanted the whispers that followed me on a daily basis to be louder than they already were. Mercifully, Celine had given up her stalking for the moment, which made my life more bearable.

"I'll make sure I take extra good notes," Eva said over breakfast.

"Huh?" I stared at her, trying to process the words into something my brain could actually understand. I hadn't slept much the night before. At all, in fact.

"In classes today. I'll make sure you don't miss anything."

I snorted into my coffee. "I think I can afford to miss half a day."

The disapproving brow raise she gave me suggested she knew exactly how far behind I really was. Maybe I just wasn't cut out for the educational system. Book learning hadn't really been my strength growing up. Nor had the more practical stuff. Or applying myself at all, really. I guess all that time in Micah's shadow— *Micah.* I shook my head, banishing the train of thought before it could take hold, and forced something that felt like a smile but was probably closer to a grimace.

"Thank you for being a good friend and making sure my dumb arse doesn't fail before they've had time to kick me out."

She shrugged. "I take my best friend duties seriously."

I couldn't help smiling at the little hair flip she did. The mood died when I felt someone's gaze on me. I turned to find Zachary standing near our table. He wore his black-trimmed cloak over his uniform and looked mildly amused at the fact he was yet again in my orbit. Mercifully, Eva said nothing, although I did feel the thump of her foot against mine. We'd had a bet going about which enforcer would be assigned to take me to the trial. I'd kept insisting there was no way it would be him. I wasn't as amused by it now as I had been when we'd been laughing and joking two weeks ago in our dorm. Zachary being here meant it was real. It was happening.

"Are you ready to go?" He kept his arms tightly clasped behind his back, ever the strong fighter type.

I didn't want to be ready. The day was finally here, and I was more of a mess inside than I had any right to be. It wasn't my trial. No one was judging me or punishing me, but I couldn't shake the feeling that today carried some level of control over my future.

"Guess so," I mumbled into my mug, and downed the rest of its contents.

"Good luck," Eva offered, and grabbed my hand, giving it a squeeze.

I had no idea how we were going to get to Circle headquarters. Bevan had said he'd arrange 'transportation'—not a portal, which was how magic users normally got around, assuming, of course, one of them knew how to conjure a portal. And it seemed a pretty safe bet that Zachary did, given that he'd passed his training as an enforcer. And still, Bevan hadn't used the word portal.

"You don't have to be nervous," Zachary said as we marched through the entry hall and into the crisp afternoon air.

"I'd be less nervous if I knew how we were getting there."

He flashed me a confident smirk and held out his hand. Internally, I both recoiled at the gesture and leapt at the fact he was offering physical contact. It was one thing to offer snarky banter, but that's all it had been. Right?

"Look, I get that having enforcers on the grounds makes you uncomfortable. You aren't the only person to have those feelings. But we're just doing our job."

"Did I say anything about that?"

"You're kind of easy to read," he said, and produced a

small stone that looked similar to the one Kelsey had given me on my last visit to the Circle, except this one was pure white.

"What is that?" I asked.

"A transportation stone. Normally, we'd portal, but security has been tightened up for the trial, and after the…events of last year."

When the druid council had been attacked in their headquarters by a rogue pack of shifters. Zachary didn't have to spell it out. They were expecting trouble today. I guess they weren't so arrogant as to think they were invincible anymore. Or maybe they were, and they were just taking precautions to show the rest of us everything that had happened was barely an inconvenience.

"Hold on tight and remember to breathe," Zachary said as the stone ignited, burning white-hot in his hand.

I cringed, anticipating pain that never came. Instead, my equilibrium ceased to exist. Up became left, down became backwards, and my lungs forgot how to function. His reminder to breathe only really registered in my head once I crashed into something firm, but not hard. I blinked as the light died around us and found myself leaning against Zachary on the front steps to the Circle's headquarters.

"Take a minute," he said, his voice a whisper in my ear.

"I think...I'm going to be sick," I gurgled, and bent double over the nearby bushes.

By some minor miracle, breakfast remained inside my body and the nausea passed. Zachary didn't look annoyed or irritated at my reaction. In fact, he looked almost concerned.

"You forgot to breathe," he commented as he hefted the large front door open.

"Arsehole," I muttered. I didn't bother to point out it was hard to breathe when the whole world turned upside down—because apparently he'd managed it. Somehow.

Instead of heading up the spiral stairs, Zachary led me straight back through a hidden panel in a wall I hadn't discovered on my first unauthorised exploration. We climbed a less terrifying set of stairs, past three landings to the large circular chamber with doors a good fifteen feet tall and wide enough that at least four people could enter shoulder-to-shoulder. The one I'd gone in the first time I came here. There weren't as many people as I expected, and I sat where Zachary directed me. Micah was nowhere to be seen.

A figure two rows below twisted round to look up at me, and I blinked in surprise. I wasn't sure why; I should have expected to see Kelsey here. She was, after all, a member of the Circle. It may sense she'd be here when they passed judgement on my brother. Still, it was hard to think of her as one of them after she'd been so kind to me.

"Norah," she said with a small smile. "You're looking well."

I was pretty sure that was a lie, because if I looked even half as bad as I felt, then I was a mess. But it was nice of her to lie about it.

"Hey. Sorry about not staying in touch," I said, trying to distance myself from my chaperone.

"I'm sure you've been busy with classes. How are you coping? It can be overwhelming at first, but I know you'll get it."

"Uh, could be worse, I guess," I answered. "So, how does this work?" I may have grown up in the magical world, but I'd never really paid attention to the legal proceedings.

"The council will hear statements from all the affected parties and then the defendant will be able to speak in his own defence if he chooses. Then they will render judgement."

I realised in that moment I had no idea what Micah would or wouldn't say in his own defence. Did he even have one? Or had he accepted what he'd done? That sense of Micah I'd picked up in Kelsey during our first encounter seemed weaker this time. Like more time had passed. It finally clicked in my head.

"Oh, shit," I blurted. "I should have realised it sooner."

Kelsey titled her head to look back at me. "Realised what?"

"You. Micah used his power on you. I knew he'd threatened someone. I should have seen it was you when we first met."

She didn't respond to my statement. I wasn't sure how to take that. Did she blame me for being so wrapped up in my own drama to not see the pain she'd been in? Or was she used to people not noticing things like that?

"You're going to speak." It came out as a statement rather than a question.

"I am." After a beat, she added, "I'm sorry. I wish things were different. And for what it's worth, I don't blame him for what he did. It wasn't his fault, not completely. Anyway, I should get going. It was nice to see you and I'm sure we'll see each other later."

She left her seat and descended to the floor of the chamber. I watched as the council members began filtering in. I spotted the woman who'd told me I had no choice but to attend Braeseth, and the Head Councilman who'd tried to silence me with magic.

"Head Councilman Cauldwell looks stressed," Zachary commented off-handedly. As if he knew I had no idea of that prick's name.

"Looks arrogant and uptight to me," I retorted.

The immense doors closed, and I turned to see Micah being ushered into the centre of the room. He looked paler than I'd last seen him. His pale blue hair was mussed, although that had always been his style choice. He thought it made him look cool. The colour was natural, not a dye job, and had been the reason behind my own ill-fated dye attempts. Still trying to be like him in some small way, after all this time. As if this was something to aspire to.

As the lights rose, casting us in the warm glow of a wreath of what looked like legit fireballs, I spotted my parents seated in the front row on the other side of the room. At least I didn't have to deal with their running commentary through the whole proceeding.

"Micah Sheehan, you are charged with fomenting rebellion and acts of violence in violation of magical law," Cauldwell began. "Today, we will hear evidence and render judgement in accordance with precedent for such offences."

Micah stood straight; his hands bound in front of him. I looked closer and I could see his fingers were trembling. I'd never known my brother to be scared of anything. Even if he was facing a harsh sentence for his part in the attempted coup. I leaned over and whispered to Zachary, "Those are some sort of magic repressing cuffs, aren't they?"

"Yes. Can't very well have the prisoners using their powers to escape."

Eva would call that barbaric and antiquated. I still had mixed emotions. I didn't want Micah to be tempted to try to hurt anyone to escape. That would just make everything worse. But he was still my big brother, and seeing him helpless like that made my stomach turn.

"The Council calls its first witness," intoned a man whose name plate read Councilman Hutton.

I disliked him from the moment he opened his mouth. From his haughty expression to his stupid combover, he reeked of bureaucracy and self-importance. I wondered what smell he'd give off to Eva if he were lying.

Kelsey stepped into the witness box and my imagined olfactory inquiry vanished. Micah had actually hurt her with what he'd done. If they were going to call anyone, it would be her. She could literally hold his fate in her hands.

"You may give your statement," Hutton said and waved Kelsey on.

Kelsey leaned forward, locking eyes with my brother. "I want to start by saying I don't blame you, Micah. You were trying to do the right thing, and I know it isn't always easy to know what that is, especially when you have someone else whispering in your ear, filling you with this belief that you were doing what was best. Older and wiser people than you were taken in by Raphael's promises, and I know it might not be what everyone wants to hear, but it's the truth. But you went about change the wrong way and people got hurt."

I turned my attention to the council members. Most of them wore surprised expressions. They'd probably expected Kelsey to give some emotional speech about how he'd threatened her life, forced her to do unspeakable acts. Yet, she was sympathising with him. She was humanising him. She was a far better person than me.

"You have to atone for your actions, and I don't know if you regret what you did, but I believe on some level that you must, and I think that should be taken into account."

Hutton cleared his throat, and I could see from the look on his face that Kelsey's words hadn't made her any friends here.

"That's all very touching, *Miss* Winters, but you are here to explain the events of the day you were so regrettably attacked to the council, not to theorise excuses for the accused."

The way Hutton emphasised 'miss' instead of using Kelsey's official title made me wonder if her friends here had been a little thin on the ground to start with. It was clear Hutton didn't feel all warm and glowy towards her.

He began to question her in great detail, drawing out the details of every horrific thing my brother had done that day—using his power on Kelsey and attacking her friends, attempting to destroy a druid academy with a device given to them by their mysterious benefactor, and then attacking its professors to escape when he'd first been caught. What had Micah been thinking? How could he have been that stupid, to think he could ever get away with something like that?

Eventually, Kelsey was dismissed from the stand, and the next witness called—a druid by the name of Dylan Griffiths, who'd been there when Raphael had made his last stand inside one of the druid academies. When Micah had stood alongside him, attacking the students, battling them. Dylan made it clear he didn't share Kelsey's faith in Micah's potential to be rehabilitated. The druid was outright hostile, and I thought I knew why. More than one druid had lost their life in that battle, if the rumours were true. But Micah hadn't been the one to take any of them. He wasn't a killer.

Eventually, he, too, was dismissed, and a steady stream of witnesses took his place, most with only a few words to say, until the day wore late into the afternoon, and my mum was pale and leaning into my father for support.

At last, there were no more witnesses to call.

Hutton gestured to Micah. "Does the defendant wish to make a statement?"

Micah shuffled forward; his hands now balled into tight fists. I imagined the edges of his nails digging into the meat of his palms to keep his hands from shaking. He wouldn't want to show weakness in front of the druids. He'd never known when to back down from a fight.

"I stand by my actions," he said.

A few gasps echoed in the room. Mostly from where my parents sat. No doubt they'd come expecting to somehow get him acquitted. I didn't have any such illusions. He would pay some price for his actions.

"Very well," Hutton replied and glanced over at Cauldwell, who gave a nod. "The Council is prepared to render judgement."

I pivoted to Zachary again. "Don't they have to like deliberate or something?"

"What makes you think they haven't already? They didn't come into this blind. They knew what statements were going to be made."

They'd pre-judged him. Even if he'd given an impassioned speech about being led astray by a bad influence, they'd already made up their minds. I guess we just had to pray that their punishment fit the crime.

Head Councilman Cauldwell cleared his throat, and all eyes in the room moved to him.

"Micah Sheehan, you are hereby sentenced to thirty years in Daoradh." The wail that went up was definitely my mother. "Further, you will have your powers bound with immediate effect. You will no longer be permitted to use your abilities."

"Bullshit," I snarled, and was halfway to my feet when Zachary's hand wrenched my left arm so hard my arse slammed back into the seat.

Micah looked stricken at the punishment. I suspected he'd anticipated some prison time. But thirty years in the highest security druid prison? That wasn't fair. It wasn't right. Eva's theory of rehabilitation was starting to sound pretty damn good right about now. Anger roiled in my belly as they led Micah away.

"I need to talk to him," I said and climbed over Zachary's legs.

"You can't. He's not permitted contact with outsiders while he's in transit," he said, on his feet in a flash and hurrying after me.

"He's my brother. I deserve to say goodbye," I hissed and shouldered my way through the small crowd that had gathered near the door to watch his exit.

"Micah!" My voice rang out and he turned to look at me. "I'm sorry."

He gave me a small, sad smile that brought hot tears to my eyes. I didn't let them fall. He mouthed 'watch your back' before being led away.

"I'd hoped they would be more lenient," Kelsey's voice sounded from beside me.

"They could have seen that he was a victim, too. They should have helped him," I spat, and stormed out of the chamber.

I didn't want to be around these people. I didn't want to be around anyone, for that matter. Just the thought of going back to the academy made me want to punch things. Something told me these stone walls would win if we went a few rounds. Zachary appeared among the throng and I stalked farther down the corridor.

"You aren't going to run away," he said and closed the gap between us in a few strides.

"I'm not going back there."

"Sure you are. But I could be convinced to make a detour before we go."

"Like what?"

"Dinner."

"Like a date?" *Why the hell would I even say that?*

He made a sound akin to a strangled cat and covered his mouth with his hand. "More like you look like you need something deep fried and I happen to know a decent pub not far from here."

"Fine," I scowled. "But you're buying."

He gave a flourish and a bow and ushered me back to the front of the building. As we stepped into the late afternoon sunlight, I remembered that today was supposed to be a celebration of magic and its history. I wasn't in the mood to celebrate. And I couldn't shake my brother's warning to watch my back.

Chapter Ten

I may have taken more time than necessary eating my fish and chips before letting Zachary bring me back to academy grounds. He'd paid for the food and reassured me about a dozen times it wasn't a date. He was contractually obligated to ensure my well-being while off grounds, which naturally involved feeding me.

The air on campus was heavy as I headed for the dorms. I expected the avoidance and the general shunning, but the way everyone literally stopped speaking when I walked by was new. Eva sat on her bed, nose shoved in her energy manipulation textbook when I threw myself at own bed.

"They're binding his powers and he's locked up for thirty years," I mumbled into my pillow.

"I heard," she said softly.

That got my attention. I sat up and looked at her. She wouldn't meet my gaze. "How do you know?"

"Everyone knows, Norah. Word travels fast around here. Most people were cheering, saying he should have got life or worse. It's barbaric."

"For once, I agree with you," I said.

"There's this party that's happening tonight. Like a rave or something," she commented after a few moments of awkward silence. "Like, you know, for Halloween."

"Yeah, because I want to spend extra time with people who hate me for no rational reason with booze," I grumbled.

"Yeah, it did sound pretty dumb." She averted her gaze.

I thought I caught a hint of disappointment in her tone. *Since when did she want to mingle in crowds?* She had as healthy a dislike of our classmates as I did. Her desire to be social rubbed me the wrong way. A voice in the back of my head said she was trying to abandon me, leaving me to fend for myself completely. But that was ridiculous. We were teenagers. Wanting to party was practically in our DNA.

"I mean, you don't have to not go just because I'd rather be anywhere else," I said in what I hoped was a conciliatory tone.

"No. You have a point. They aren't big fans of me either and putting alcohol in the mix isn't going to make that better." After a beat, she propped her chin on her right hand. "So, what was it like spending a whole day with your boyfriend off grounds?"

"Shut up. He's not my boyfriend." The fact I'd asked if our meal on the way back was a date would seem to indicate I had other expectations. Well, they could sod right off. "He got us there with this absolute torture device. I mean, like whoever invented this transportation stone thing is a right wanker."

"Sounds unpleasant," she agreed, wrinkling her nose for effect.

"And I guess it could have been worse seeing my brother sentenced to spend the next three decades locked up. I could have had to watch it sitting with my parents, pretending to believe in their outrage. So, I guess having Zachary there made it less hostile. And he bought me food afterward."

"You're trying to pretend that wasn't a date, aren't you?"

I chuckled. "I may have asked that very question. The look on his face, it looked like he'd sucked the sourest lemon on the planet. I must repulse him. So, no, definitely not a date."

Eva leaned back against the wall behind her bed, flexing her hands as she made little bluish green sparks jump from hand to hand. She was getting much better at that. I settled with the pillow pressed against my chest. "I suppose there's a way we could find out."

She cocked her head to the side. "Find out what?"

I chucked the pillow at her, regretting it as the scent of burnt fabric filled the space between us. "Whether he finds me repulsive, duh."

"I am not a human lie detector," she protested when my meaning registered, and tossed the soiled pillow on the spare bed.

"But you kind of are. Come on, be honest. You're more curious than I am."

"And if I agreed to this, which I haven't yet, where would we even find him?"

Already know I was going to regret this, I replied, "How much you want to bet this party is semi sanctioned. I have to believe they wouldn't let a bunch of horny teenagers all sneak out to celebrate Halloween, and get absolutely bladdered when half of them don't have much more control over their magic than me."

"You think he's going to be at the party?"

"There's only one way to know for sure."

Eva threw her head back and laughed. Her whole body shook and I glared at her, waiting for the moment to pass.

"What's so funny?" I snapped.

"Oh, just that all it took to get you to change your mind about going to the party was the possibility that Zachary would be there."

"I'm not going for the ambiance or the vibe or whatever. It's purely for research purposes. Not having a unique ability of my own, I want to help you hone yours. Let me live vicariously through you."

"Right. Well, if we're going to this thing, we're both going to need a wardrobe change."

* * *

I'd never have pegged Eva for having expert fashion sense. Don't get me wrong, she dressed nice, but I'd seen her in on weekends, living in her comfy jeans and baggy jumpers. Yet somehow, she'd unearthed not one but two pair of perfectly fitting skinny jeans and light-weight jumpers that hung off the shoulder in shades of deep magenta and burgundy. Both looked amazing on her. I'd taken the magenta one out of fear that the burgundy would be perceived as too close to red. I didn't need people thinking I was projecting anger.

"Okay, I bow to your powers of make-over," I said when I looked back at my smoky eye make-up in the mirror. It was just noticeable enough to be alluring and matched the hues of the clothing in such an uncanny fashion I almost believed she'd manipulated it.

"I like to be girly sometimes," she said with a shrug. She'd twisted her hair into elegant plaits that crisscrossed around her head and wore silver teardrop earrings.

"Right, so you remember the plan?" I said, blotting a touch of lip gloss off with a sheet of toilet paper.

She heaved an exaggerated sigh. "Yes, Norah, I remember the plan. We find Zachary, you get all flirty and see what he says. I tell you if he's lying."

"The faster we find him, the faster we get out," I added.

"Right."

Having run out of reasons to stall, we traipsed through the empty halls down to the entryway. I half-expected instructors to be lined up to scold us for a night of teenage debauchery, but no one was around. Still, I stopped short of the front doors. Something felt *off*.

"What's wrong?" Eva asked in a hushed tone that still managed to bounce around noisily in the space.

"I don't know," I muttered. I wanted to ignore my paranoia, but I couldn't shake the sense that whatever was bothering me, it was better to confront it. "You go ahead. I'll catch up to you."

Eva hooked her arm through mine and gave my hand a squeeze. "Whatever's going on, you're starting to give off this weird sort of smoky smell. So, I'm not going anywhere."

I wasn't sure whether to be offended that my best friend had told me I smelled or if I was starting to veer subconsciously into lying territory. Part of me didn't want to find out. Besides, I wasn't opposed to having back-up. I looked around the empty entry hall, unsure what had drawn my attention.

Slowly, something like a slithering shadow passed along the floor, heading the direction of Dean Bevan's office. That couldn't be good. I swallowed the lump of fear in my throat that was making it painful to breathe, and marched forward, dragging Eva along with me.

"What are we doing?" she hissed when we reached the door. I didn't have an answer. A tiny sliver of pale light peeked out from beneath the door. I didn't want to look like a complete fool barging into the dean's office, but the door was already open. It swung inward at the lightest touch from my hand. The office was empty. So at least we wouldn't have to deal with Bevan losing it at us for hassling him after hours.

But why did I come here?

I shuffled backward and stopped when I felt something like a hand brushing against the nape of my neck. I spun, pulling my arm free of Eva's grip. No one was there, but that same slithering shadow darted into the auditorium. I took one step closer and picked up on the sound of low voices engaged in some sort of argument.

"Maybe we should just forget whatever this is," Eva hissed in my ear.

"I won't be offended if you bolt," I told her as I snuck closer to the doors. The closer I got, the more convinced I became I recognised the voices.

"Would you stop?" Celine's voice said in a harsh snap.

Of course it would have something to do with her. I should have known. She hadn't been making my existence painful recently. I was due for some bitchy misery to be bestowed upon me. Knowing who was behind the door made my desire to turn and run spike. My heart hammered against my ribs, and my palms went slick with sweat. If Eva could pick up on a person's nerves, too, she was probably about to get sick from the level of anxiety coursing through me.

"Norah," Eva hissed, and made a grab for my hand as I pushed the doors open, leaving her out of view. It was safer if they thought I was alone.

"I didn't think the party was in here," I said loudly, making my presence abundantly clear.

One of Celine's cronies—I think her name was Jessa, or was it Miranda—spun so fast I wouldn't have been surprised if her head kept going to make a thirty hundred and sixty degree rotation. "It's not. Get out!"

"Don't be so rude, Miranda," Celine said.

Miranda jabbed a finger at me. "She's not supposed to even be in here. She made it clear she's not interested in what's really going on. She's a stupid little sheep like the rest of them."

To say literal sparks flew from Celine's outstretched fingers was an understatement. Thick bolts of electricity raced up Miranda's arms and wrapped around her mouth like a gag. "Shut up."

The other girl—Jessa, I assumed, by process of elimination—looked terrified and took a step back from

119

Celine.

Celine turned, her obnoxious red hair fanning out behind her. "I know what happened to your brother. It was barbaric and wrong. He was fighting for something real. He should be free, don't you think?"

"You keep talking about my brother like you knew him," I said coldly, narrowing my eyes at her. "Like he would have given two shits about you. The truth is, he wouldn't even have looked twice at you."

I was so tired of her acting like she knew anything about me or my life. She kept talking about wanting to change things, to pick up his cause, but Micah didn't have a cause. Not really. He'd been swept up in someone else's feverish rhetoric. He'd brought into the cult, and he was paying a far heavier price than he deserved. But that didn't mean I was going to join their crusade. I wasn't going to make the same mistakes he did.

Celine turned to face me now, her hands still crackling with lightning looking for somewhere to strike. "You really should just get out of here, Norah. Go to the party, get wasted, make out with one of those druid lapdogs."

How does she know about Zachary?

I hated myself for thinking that at all. There nothing to know. He'd just been doing his job escorting me today. And sure, he'd been polite to me on a few occasions, but I wasn't under any illusions that he was anything more to me than security. I was someone he had to keep an eye on.

"Whatever you're planning, just remember that you aren't going to get away with it," I said. My tone carried far more bravado than I felt.

Celine threw her head back and laughed. I could see all of her teeth and for a moment I pictured some of them having elongated points. When she looked back at me, I could see the flickers of power reflected in her irises. Or at least the slivers of them not taken up by her pupils.

"You really think I'm afraid of you? Little Miss Can't-Do-Magic?" She stepped closer, and I could feel the hairs on the backs of my forearms prickling in response to her power. "You think people don't notice, but I do. You suck at magic. We've been here two months and you can barely get a spark to ignite."

Anger washed over me like the flashpoint in a fire, unexpected and sucking all the air from my lungs. It wasn't her words, it was that she was the one who'd said them. I'd thought them to myself plenty of times since coming here. But that was my own self-loathing. *I* was allowed to think I was shit at this whole magic thing. But this girl who I'd never done anything to, she didn't have that right. And she didn't have the right to talk about my brother.

I didn't realise it was happening until someone let out a shriek. At first, nothing strange registered in my brain. The room looked a little darker, maybe, but that wasn't something that should cause someone to freak out.

"Get it off of me!" Jessa whined.

I turned to see her trying and failing to bat away coiling wisps of shadows as they snaked up her legs and up her torso. I looked to Celine to find her pinned to the nearest seat, her arms out straight in front of her, fingers splayed so she couldn't conjure electricity.

"You're hurting me," Jessa howled.

My brow furrowed as I looked at my own hands. The same shadowy tendrils that were encasing her body were flowing from my palms.

"Oh, shit." I shook my hands, hoping it would end whatever spell I'd somehow conjured, but it only fuelled the shadows to consume her faster.

"Stop it," Celine ground out through a clenched jaw.

"I'm trying," I rasped, this time balling my hands into tight fists in the hopes that might quench the hunger feeding the power.

My ears barely registered the thunder of footsteps entering the room and I had no sense of who was there until I felt a pair of strong hands wrap around mine, pressing something damp and smelling of pine against my fingers. It stuck my fingers together like sap and made my skin itch so that I wanted to claw at it. But somehow it tamped down on the spell so that the dark magic receded. I craned my neck to see Zachary standing behind me. He'd stopped the spell. I caught sight of Eva standing just outside the doorway, looking paler than I'd ever seen her.

What the bloody hell had just happened?

Chapter Eleven

I expected dozens of enforcers to come pouring in, to throw shackles on me and haul me off somewhere. Instead, only one other enforcer appeared, the one who'd led us to our dorms on the first night. I'd forgotten her name—or maybe I never knew it. It wasn't like I'd been trying to make friends with them. She helped Celine and Jessa up. Miranda's lips were puckered with nasty burns. At least I knew that hadn't been my doing. Celine was even more twisted than I'd thought, to do that to one of her own friends.

My hands ached beneath the balm Zachary had slapped on them to stop the shadows from doing whatever the hell they'd been about to do, and I held them awkwardly out in front of me, terrified of ruining Eva's clothes. I wanted to speak, to apologise, to tell them they shouldn't have interfered... Something, anything, but it was like my voice had been silenced when the darkness had receded.

"The healers will get you sorted," the female enforcer said to Celine and her friends as she and Zachary escorted us to the medwing, and true enough, once we arrived, several healers bustled over to them.

Zachary led Eva and me to a pair of beds further down the ward and pulled a curtain. He gestured to a tray with a waiting row of cloths and then said to Eva, "Hand me one of those."

She did so, and I could see her fingers tremble. Zachary slowly began wiping the sap from my hands. As he cleared the substance away, my skin burned from its sudden exposure to air. I winced and instinctively pulled my hands back.

"I know it's unpleasant, but it's better if I get it all off quickly," he said, his tone soft.

"How'd you find us?" Talking was a good distraction, and right now I needed something to distract me from the itching and the burning, and the knowledge of what I'd almost done.

"Your friend had the presence of mind to get help," he answered.

"I'm sorry. Everything went sort of darky and smoky and I panicked," she offered.

"Don't apologise. I uh...I couldn't have stopped without help."

"Want to tell me what you were doing in there in the first place?" Zachary's tone shifted from protector to interrogator, and I stared down at my hands. The exposed skin was red and throbbed painfully.

"Nothing illegal," I said, not missing the defensive tone in my own voice. I tried to take it down a notch. "We were just talking and things got out of hand."

I caught Eva mouth the word 'smoke'. It wasn't that big of a lie. Hell, it was basically true.

"I would have thought they'd have been down at the party," he said, setting the cloth aside.

I tilted my head as I took in his words. He'd definitely said 'they', not 'you' or 'you all'. So, he hadn't expected me to be there. Behind him, Eva waved her hands and made kissy lips. I fought to keep from rolling my eyes. Now was so not the time to figure out if he liked me.

"Yeah, well, parties suck, and people are arseholes," I said.

"You look like you were heading there yourself," he commented.

Heat crept up the nape of my neck. "I mean, I figured it would be chaperoned or whatever so it couldn't be that crazy."

"Only had to put out two bonfires gone rogue," he said with a small smirk.

"Oh."

I could read on Eva's face that she wasn't pleased with me dodging our original objective in attending the party. "So, do you think it's too late for us to go?" I blurted.

"What?" Zachary's gaze flitted from me to Eva and back again.

"I just meant for me and Eva," I clarified hastily.

"You know, because Eva got dressed up and everything."

He glanced at her, and made no comment on the fact I was also dressed up.

"I'm afraid no one else is going to the party. It's been shut down. Besides, the dean is going to want to talk to you."

"When?"

"Once everyone's checked out and cleared."

"So, like now? But that's got to be against academy rules or something. It's after hours."

"Now you want to talk about academy rules?" He arched a brow at me and I flushed red. Yeah, I was pretty sure attacking another student with life-sucking shadows was breaking a fairly major rule.

He grasped my hands in his and I felt them warm beneath his touch. "Be honest with me. Was that really the first time you've ever done something like that?"

"Yes!" He searched my eyes, and I fought the urge to squirm, look away, or move closer. I sucked in a breath. "I swear, I have no idea what happened or how I did that."

He pulled his hands away and I hated him for it. His touch had made the chaos swirling inside me settle down. And then I hated myself for needing someone to do that for me. Needing people wasn't who I was. I stared at my hands again. The redness was fading. "What was that stuff you put on my hands?"

"A neutralising agent. It suppresses your magic. I'm sorry, I know it's unpleasant."

That statement sent a shiver down my spine. I didn't want to know why or how long he'd had that on him. Was it a precaution he'd bought along for our day in court? Had he expected he'd need to use it earlier?

"I'm going to check on the other girls. Once everyone is cleared to leave, I'll take you to see the dean," Zachary said before ducking around the curtain, leaving me and Eva alone.

"I meant what I said earlier," I said before she could speak. "Thank you for getting help."

She bit her lip and looked down at the ground.

"I've never seen anything like that, Norah. What was that?"

"I don't know. She was just talking shit about me, and I know I do that about myself all the time, but something just flipped this switch in me. I wanted them all to be quiet and back off, and the next thing I knew, there were these shadow things coming out of my hands. I couldn't stop it. I tried, Eva, I swear I tried to stop it."

"It sounds like a manifestation event," she whispered.

I shook my head. "No way. That doesn't happen this late. It's like a puberty thing." I gestured to my body. "And that already happened."

"All I'm saying is what it looked like to me. When it happened to me, I lost control, too," she replied.

If she was right, then I'd just discovered a unique power after all. And if that was the case, it changed *everything*. I had more magic inside of me than anyone thought, and I could wield it. If I could figure out how the hell it came out of me—and more importantly, how to stop it. Because this power made me dangerous.

"Do you think Dean Bevan is going to be pissed?" I whispered, rubbing my hands along my thighs. They were tingling rather than burning now.

"I mean, it was an accident. And it's not like anyone really got hurt," she said.

"What made you get Zachary?"

"I told you, I kind of freaked and figured someone in authority should know what was going on."

"Right, but you could have found anyone."

She sighed. "Maybe I was still curious to know if I said you were in trouble, if he'd drop everything and come." She leaned in. "For what it's worth, he did."

I couldn't hide the smile that stretched across my lips. "Did you happen to ask if he liked me?"

She rolled her eyes and settled on the bed beside me. "Didn't really have time with everything going on—you know, the whole black shadow of doom thing kind of lent some urgency to the situation. And it's not like you tried very hard just now."

"Well, excuse me for being kind of freaked out, too."

"How'd you burn what's-her-name's mouth?"

I shook my head. "That was Celine. I don't know what they were plotting but Celine clearly wanted Miranda to shut up. It's like she turned the lightning into a living thing that obeyed her command."

Eva bumped my shoulder in solidarity. "You've got your own living shadow thing going for you now, so she's not that scary."

"I don't know about that. She was plenty scary and in case you missed it, I can't exactly control this shadow thing."

"You'll learn. And look at it this way, now we have even more homework to do together."

I snickered and couldn't hide a smile. Maybe this wasn't such a terrible thing. Unless, of course, Dean Bevan saw fit to chuck me out of the academy for attacking a fellow student. Or...well, they wouldn't lock me up for what just happened, would they? I mean, it had been an accident, not like what Micah had done. As if reading my mind, Zachary pulled the curtain aside and beckoned me onward. I looked to Eva one last time for support before following his lead out of the infirmary. To my surprise, Celine and her cronies were still receiving treatment.

"This is bad, isn't it?" I said, my voice barely a whisper, as we navigated the corridors back to the first floor and Bevan's office.

The fact Zachary didn't answer my question spoke volumes, whether he realised it or not. I'd got so wrapped up in whether he liked me that his silence stung more than it should. Probably more than he meant it to. And I needed to hurry up and get my emotions straight, because, like it or not, he was an enforcer. He was here to make sure I didn't break the law, nothing more. And I'd just done exactly that.

Crossing through the entry hall made my stomach twist into constricting knots. Up in the infirmary I could pretend I wasn't going to go before the dean in the dead of night alone with no real defence of what I'd been doing in the auditorium in the first place. But this was real. I had done that; I had conjured those shadows to attack Celine and her friends, and now I was going to have to pay the price for it. How heavy a price would they demand?

I stopped short of entering Bevan's office, like my body refused to go any further. Zachary turned to face me.

"It's better to get it over with. Trust me."

The way he emphasised the last two words tugged at my attention and my brain spiralled down an infinite chasm of the true meaning and intent of his words.

"I'm scared," I whispered. Braeseth was compulsory, but surely people got expelled—and bound. *What would happen then?* With the drama surrounding Micah, my parents probably wouldn't notice me back at home, but I couldn't stay under their roof forever. Maybe I could find a job doing something mundane and non-magical. Two months ago, it would have sounded like bliss.

Forcing myself forward, I crossed the threshold back into Dean Bevan's office. It felt strange to be in there again after my little detour before confronting Celine. Had whatever weird shadow magic I'd done been guiding me? Bevan was sitting behind the desk, much as he had when he'd given me permission to attend Micah's trial. This time the dark bags under his eyes and the haggard expression betrayed him as a man in need of sleep and maybe a break. From us.

"Sit down, Miss Sheehan," he said, gesturing to the chair opposite him.

Zachary took up residence guarding the door. Or barring my exit. No matter what was coming, he wasn't giving me any choice in the matter. He had at least five years on me and a sizable amount of muscle, not to mention the magical skill that came with years of training at the elite enforcer academy. The only way past him was if he decided to move.

I sat on the edge of the chair, clenching and flexing my hands to try to work some of the anxiety out of my system. Bevan's right eye twitched with every movement of my fingers, and I realised it must look like I was preparing to unleash whatever the shadow thing was. I swallowed hard and sat on my hands instead. Immediately, my feet started trying to flex, like they wanted me to make a run for it—into the brick wall of an enforcer blocking my only escape.

"Look, if you're going to chuck me out, just do it," I said, fixing my gaze on a swirling blue orb on a shelf behind Bevan.

"I'm not going to expel you," he replied. His tone was indignant. Like I had the gall to expect him to throw me out.

I turned my attention back to him. "You're not? But the thing I did... isn't that like an expulsion-level offence? Or... worse?"

Bevan steepled his fingers beneath his chin. "What you experienced is a manifestation event, Miss Sheehan." I glared at him. Clearly, he thought I was stupid.

"So people keep saying," I muttered sullenly.

"It is not a crime or against the rules for one's magic to manifest. It is a natural process. Granted, we usually expect to see such revelation of one's unique magic long before you enter our halls, though given the nature of the event, we should perhaps consider ourselves fortunate."

Shit, he was right. That could have happened at home. Around my family. With no-one to stop it.

"Why am I different?"

He shook his head. "I can't say. But now that it has made itself known, you will be expected to attend unique magics with your classmates."

"I'd already be months behind," I protested.

"I'm sorry, it is non-negotiable."

He didn't sound sorry. He sounded more than a little like Head Councilman Cauldwell—imperious and condescending.

"I didn't ask for this," I ground out and lunged to my feet. My hands ached and the edges of my vision grew dark, like shadows were creeping in. Scrunching my eyes shut, I took a deep breath and blew it out slowly.

"That may be, but it is my job to ensure the students who pass through this academy receive a quality education. Failing to provide with you training on how to control your magic would be a dereliction of my duty."

"Can I go now?"

"Yes." After a pause he added, "Oh, I thought you might want to know that your brother's powers were successfully bound. No problems at all."

I did my best to mask my horror at the thought of my brother losing access to his magic. Maybe it was because it seemed such an unfair punishment for what he'd done, or maybe because I now had a unique power of my own, I saw how foolish I'd been, begging the Circle to bind my powers. Zachary stepped out of the doorway and let me pass before falling into step beside me.

"I don't need an escort," I snapped.

"You may think Bevan missed it, but I saw how close you came to losing it in there," he said, shoving his hands in his pockets. His words said he didn't trust me but his posture said he wasn't worried. *God, confusing much?*

"Maybe *you* missed it, but I *did* control it."

"Look, you won't be that far behind, and you seem close to your roommate. Can't she help you get caught up?" he said as we headed up the stairs to the dorms.

"I can't put all that on Eva. That's not fair to her." I also had no doubt she'd offer in a heartbeat.

"Can't hurt to ask," he said with a shrug. As we reached the second floor, he continued. "Don't you want to have control?"

"I guess," I replied.

"I couldn't stand feeling like the power controlled me," he said softly. His expression went wistful, like he was recalling some unknown time he wasn't in control.

I couldn't picture him being out of control of anything. He'd been so calm when I'd gone all darkness and doom. He'd known exactly how to reach me, how to help. He'd been comforting.

"You've never been out of control," I scoffed, knowing full well I had zero idea if it was true.

"You'd be surprised," he said. His lips pressed into a frown, but he didn't elaborate.

We reached the first year dorms and he gestured to the archway. "Get some sleep and rest up before classes start up again. Trust me, you'll feel better after some downtime."

I wanted to trust him. I still didn't have the courage to ask him why he kept showing up in my orbit. "Thanks again for you know…" I waved my hands at him.

"It's my job." I caught the slight pause as he chose his words. What other word had he been about to say?

I didn't have time to ask before he darted down the hall. With a sigh, I retreated to the dorm to find Eva already asleep. I changed into my nightclothes and crawled beneath the covers, welcoming the shadows, natural shadows this time, around me, urging them to lull me to sleep. Maybe he was right, and sleep would make things clearer.

Or maybe the shadows would swallow me whole.

Chapter Twelve

Hiding out in the dorm until Monday was harder than I thought. It was probably all in my head, but I swear I could hear voices carrying through the archway from other dorms, accusing me of assaulting Celine and her friends. I knew their opinions shouldn't matter, but I wasn't convinced I hadn't done some lasting damage to them.

"I know I'm the last person to give you advice on dealing with people," Eva said as we claimed our seats in Rathbone's class, "but even if you did hurt Celine, they all know she probably deserved it. She's kind of a bitch."

"But I don't want to hurt people, not even ones who do deserve it," I replied, slumping in my chair. I'd bet that was how Micah had started out, lashing out at people who'd wronged him, and it never ended there. I glanced at Eva as she pulled out her notes from the last week's lesson. I hadn't even remembered were supposed to be doing an assignment.

"I don't know how he expects me to pass any of these classes. So, I've got a unique magic, big deal."

"I already told you a million times this weekend, I'm going to help you get caught up. And not just in unique magics," she replied.

That was all good and well, but we both knew that I'd

missed two whole months of very practical training in unique magics. And that might not have been a problem for someone who was naturally gifted with their magic...but nothing about magic had ever come naturally to me. *Except the shadows.* I shoved the thought aside. I didn't want the shadows to come, naturally or otherwise. They scared me. People could get hurt.

The door swung inward, and I tensed as Rathbone entered. He wasn't usually this early. His hair was completely down today and it had a slight wave to it. It made him look more like an aging hippy than ever. He settled at his desk, not paying us any attention.

"Just promise me that you won't let me drag you down," I said. "Eventually, you'll realise I'm a lost cause. Don't let your own grades suffer."

She snickered. "You're passing your classes whether you want to or not, Nor. Even if I have to drag you kicking and screaming through the whole semester."

I sat up and faced her. I didn't expect her to reach out and clap both palms on my cheeks. "And you are not a lost cause. Now, no more negative thinking. Say it with me."

"No more negative thinking?" My voice came out uncertain, and she rolled her eyes.

"Close enough."

To no one's surprise, even more people skirted the

desks around me. Celine and her gaggle arrived and claimed desks on the complete opposite side of the room. I noted that she made Jessa sit in my direct line of sight. Apparently, she was the fall person in case I lost my temper and lashed out at them. The burn marks were gone from Miranda's lips. Magic really could do wonders.

"Shouldn't she be expelled?" Rory, a guy who was all brawn and zero brain, so far as I'd been able to tell, demanded, jabbing a finger in my direction.

Rathbone stood and clapped his hands together. "Everyone who is meant to be in this class is present. So, let's focus on the lesson, shall we?"

Rory cast Celine a look that I assumed meant 'I tried' before sitting down in his seat. Celine, for her part, just flat out refused to look at me as Rathbone paced the front of the room.

"So, the last few classes we've been practicing summoning energy in larger quantities." He demonstrated by summoning a thin web of lightning that stretched from the tips of each finger on his left hand. "We're going to build on that today. The goal of today's lesson is to summon it in both hands, just along your fingers."

"Can't we just get to making energy balls already?" Rory groaned.

Rathbone pivoted to face Rory. "If I wanted you to incinerate half the campus, I'd let you go making energy balls left, right, and centre. However, seeing as none of us want that, you'll have to be patient. And if I hear of anyone trying to jump ahead in the curriculum, we're going to have problems."

Power rippled over his right hand as he spoke, the same thin web of electrons spreading out across his outstretched fingers. Even if it wasn't meant as a threat, it shut Rory up. I couldn't help smiling to myself. Rathbone clapped his hands together and the electricity vanished, as if the simple act of putting his hands together snuffed it from existence.

I straightened a little in my chair and did my best to master the skills he was teaching. I could pretty easily get the energy to manifest between my thumb and forefinger now in one hand without much effort. Getting it to spread like he'd done was harder than he made it look. Harder than most of my classmates made it look. I bit my lip in concentration and a spark leapt off the tiny branch of lightning to my middle finger. It settled on the tip of my finger and another spark shot off from it, landing on my fourth finger, and then one last time to arc to my pinky.

"I did it," I whispered to Eva, too nervous that if I said it any louder, the full force of my classmates' attention would ruin the moment.

"I keep telling you that you can," she replied. She was

turned so her back was facing me.

I caught a bluish-purple glow coming from both sides of her body. She'd likely figured it out already and didn't want me to feel embarrassed. I wasn't even mad about it. She was letting me have this little moment of triumph. She was a much better friend than I deserved.

"Good, now, try the other hand," Rathbone said, appearing beside my desk as if out of thin air.

His presence made my heart beat faster and my right hand grew slick with sweat. Water and electricity weren't generally the best mix. I wiped it off on my clothes and tried my best to replicate the results.

"You have the power within you. You just have to focus and harness it, Norah."

I closed my eyes, trying to picture what it would look like to have electricity flowing from both hands. Equal currents stretching over my skin, ready to obey me. I could see it in my mind's eye, and then I felt something ripple over my right hand.

"Norah, stop," Rathbone's voice was sharp.

I opened my eyes to see that there was no electricity dancing on my fingertips. Tiny wisps of shadow slithered around my hand, curling and unfurling in my palm. I turned to check my left hand to find the electricity had faded, replaced by shadow.

A dull ringing filled my ears and the edges of my

vision went fuzzy. Not like when I'd been in Dean Bevan's office. The kind of fuzzy that comes just before you black out.

"I can't," I murmured, my tongue thick, like it was three sizes too big for my mouth.

"Listen to me. Imagine them receding, draw them back into your body," Rathbone said.

"Come on, Norah, you can do this," Eva said in my ear.

Swallowing when my tongue felt so huge was uncomfortable, but I did, focusing on forcing the shadows to recede. I watched, transfixed, as they vanished. A knot I hadn't realised had formed between my shoulder blades ached with the effort and I slumped back against the seat.

"It was a good effort. I think you were very nearly there," Rathbone said with an encouraging smile before walking away to dismiss the rest of the class.

"He saw what happened, right? That wasn't anything like I was supposed to be doing," I grumbled, and shouldered my bag.

"I mean, it seems like your shadows are triggered like energy manipulation. Come on, let's get to unique magics. Maybe you can talk to Glover before everyone else gets there."

"Norah, a moment, please," Rathbone said, just as I

was about to slip outside the door. I shared a look with Eva.

"I'll wait for you outside," she said, and I nodded, shoulders slumping as I turned back to Rathbone.

"I'm sorry," I pre-empted. "I didn't mean for it to happen. I wasn't trying to hurt anyone. I was trying to do your exercise, and I was getting it—you saw me. I just… I don't know what happened, I…"

Rathbone held up a hand, and my tumult of words stumbled to a halt.

"You're not in any trouble," he said, and it seemed like people were telling me that everywhere I went. Except for the ones trying to get me kicked out, that was. "And that's not why I asked you to stay behind."

"It's not?"

"No. But since you brought it up, I will say, you demonstrated excellent control in preventing the shadow magic from manifesting further, especially considering you haven't had any training in how to control it yet."

"But the others—"

He shook his head, cutting me off again. I wasn't sure why I bothered trying to get a full sentence out anymore.

"You can't expect yourself to be at their level. They've had much longer to get used to their unique magics than you, and more training, too. It will take you time to get there."

Time. I nodded. And until then, I was going to have to try to keep the shadows from smothering anyone, or whatever it was they'd do if I lost control. Maybe just prevent people from getting sunburned...but somehow, I didn't think so.

"So, uh," I scuffed my feet. "If that's not what you wanted to talk to me about..."

"Why are you here?"

I nodded again.

"I know you've been through a lot recently, and I understand it must have been difficult seeing such a severe sentence handed down to your brother—"

I opened my mouth to deny it, and he pressed on right over the top of me.

"—and you're not fooling me, Norah, I can see what it's costing you. He's still your brother. No-one would blame you for having mixed feelings. It doesn't make you a traitor—to us, or to him."

"Great. Thanks. Good talk." I jerked my chin away, trying to smother the illogical anger welling up in me. "Can I go now?"

"I just want you to know that if you need someone to talk to, you can come and find me, anytime. I'm happy to be an impartial ear."

I stared at him, expressionless, and he exhaled heavily and nodded.

"Yes, you can go. Instructor Glover will be waiting."

* * *

Instructor Glover turned out to be a woman in her forties with high cheekbones and a sharply pointed nose. She wore so much eye make-up it looked like she was expecting to be on stage instead of at the front of a lecture room. Her russet curls bounced with every turn of her head.

"You must be Miss Sheehan," she said the moment I stepped into the lecture room.

After getting away from Rathbone, we'd rushed straight here, so no one else had come in, yet.

"Uh, yes, Instructor Glover," I answered.

"You're going to have quite a lot to catch up on." She handed me a syllabus.

"Given that Norah is behind, and really it's not her fault, is there anything you could to help her?" Eva asked.

Glover's piercing blue gaze travelled from my roommate's face to mine and back again. "I don't generally make a habit of giving students extra tutoring but as this is an unusual situation, I will make time Saturday morning for the next month to get you caught up."

I forced a smile and nodded before stalking to the back of the lecture room. Eva sat beside me and started unloading her notepad. "Did you have to sign me up for

Saturday morning tutoring?" I hissed.

"You wanted me to help you," she answered.

"Yeah, you. Not her. She looks like she would rather claw her own eyes out."

"She's not that bad. Trust me. If you just get to know her, you'll see that she wants everyone to succeed."

I skimmed the syllabus Glover had handed me and found that today's lesson was supposed to be about controlling our powers. Well, at least I came at a time that seemed particularly relevant to my situation.

Slowly, most of the rest of the class filtered in. I noted that Celine wasn't present. Miranda handed Glover a note before sitting down. The instructor glanced over whatever was written, made a dismissive sound, and tossed it on her desk.

"How much you want to bet Celine is wimping out because she's just too fragile," Eva said with a dramatic eye roll and pressed her hand to her forehead in a fake fainting gesture.

She hadn't seemed that traumatised in Rathbone's class, but my shadow magic had reared its ugly head again. I suppose that could have set her off. Or, more likely, she was just skipping because she thought she didn't need the help. In that moment, I decided I was going to accept whatever help Glover and the other instructors were willing to offer me. I was stuck with my magic, and I had something that was mine now. If I didn't want other people to think I was a ticking time bomb, I needed to learn to control this ability.

"Alright, everyone settle down," Glover said, clapping hers for attention. "Today we will be continuing our work on control. If you've been doing the assignments, then you should feel prepared for this lesson." She gestured for everyone to stand.

I followed everyone's lead and pushed my bag up against the wall behind me. No one looked surprised by whatever was happening. Eva grabbed my sleeve and guided me out of the path of a skittering desk. Glover had raised her hands and all the desks skated along the floor in opposite directions, crashing against the four walls to give us space to stand and work.

"Guessing that's normal," I muttered to Eva as I shuffled toward a corner. I might be accepting that I needed to learn everything the woman at the front of the class had to teach, but I still didn't need everyone's attention on me. I wasn't all that keen on getting Glover's attention, either. And if possible, I'd prefer not to get kicked out in my first lesson, in case she decided I needed to work on Sunday mornings as well—when I'd rather be sleeping.

"Most of the time. Honestly, I don't know why she just doesn't keep the desks there. I can't think of one time we've sat and taken notes."

"Warm-ups, please," Glover said, and marched toward me.

Everyone paused mid-motion and stared at me. I found Rory and glared at him, intending to flip him off, but Glover got to me before I could do it discreetly. Still, I caught him take a step back to put even more distance between us.

"Every class, we begin with warmups to get our bodies and minds prepared to harness our unique abilities," Glover said, drawing my full attention.

"Warm-ups, right. Like, um, stretches or something?"

She let out an exasperated sigh. "Just close your eyes and do as I say."

"I should warn you, the last time I closed my eyes and did something an instructor told me, my magic kind of went crazy."

"Stop talking and just listen," she snapped.

I clamped my mouth shut and let her guide me.

"Now, raise your arms out to your sides." She grabbed my wrists and yanked my arms up because apparently I wasn't responding fast enough. "Now, flex your fingers. Try to do it one finger on one hand at a time. Feel the ligaments and tendons and joints bend. Let that feeling travel all the way up your arm, across your shoulders and down the other arm."

I felt foolish standing here flexing my fingers one at a time, but I did as instructed. I wasn't sure if I was supposed to feel something specific—other than embarrassment—as I did, but I didn't notice anything enlightening. It seemed to take forever to get through each finger, but it was probably only a few minutes at most.

"Good, now, bend at the waist, let your arms hang loose in front of you," Glover said.

I cracked one eyelid to see if everyone was actually doing this. They were. Even Rory. I almost expected him to tip over from being so top heavy with muscle, but he hung limp like a ragdoll, arms and hands swaying gently in front of him. I closed my eyes again and waited for Glover to give her next instruction.

"Good, now, stand up straight slowly, feeling one vertebra align itself at a time. As you feel that alignment, take a slow, deep breath and blow it out."

By the time I'd straightened and blown out my breath, I had to admit I felt more relaxed. Was that really that important to doing magic? If it was, why didn't every instructor have us doing relaxation exercises at the start of each class?

"Now, we are going to work in twenty to thirty second concentrated bursts of power for those of you with physical manifesting abilities," she said.

Eva drifted off to a grouping of desks I hadn't realised had been formed into a square. She sat with a few other students. She cast me an apologetic look before turning to face the small cluster. Before I had time to question it, Glover was back at my side.

"So, since we have to start you from the basics, tell me about your power."

"Uh, well, it's sort of a shadow thing."

"What does it feel like when it manifests?"

"I don't know. Scary. I mean, I never mean to do it. I didn't even know I could do it," I rambled.

"No. Describe what the magic *feels* like to you when it manifests. Does it have weight, a scent, a texture?"

Heat burned a path up the nape of my neck. I should have realised that's what she meant. "Oh. I guess I never really paid attention. I was always in panic mode to make it stop."

"Well, that's your first lesson then, to pay attention and describe to me at our first tutoring session what your magic feels like. Until we understand its physical manifestations, we can't begin to train your emotional triggers."

As she walked away to tend to the other students, I tried to recall what the shadows felt like when they'd appeared each time. But no matter how hard I tried, I couldn't remember. It was like somehow the memory was blocked from me. *That can't be normal.* Across the room, I watched Eva smile at one of the girls in her little group. At least one of us was making strides.

Chapter Thirteen

Nine o'clock on a Saturday was a torturous time to be awake, but here I sat, six weeks after joining unique magics with Glover. I had to admit, I'd made more progress than I expected. I wasn't anywhere near the level of the rest of the class and Glover had begrudgingly agreed to extend our study sessions a few more weeks. But that extra help was nearly over. We were about to go off for Christmas break and when I came back, I'd be on my own.

"Explain it again," she said, sitting on the edge of her desk. Her red curls were looser today, and she'd forgone the excessive eye make-up. She looked… normal.

"It doesn't have a constant feeling. It changes. Sometimes it's like silky ribbon sliding across my skin. And sometimes it's like thick plumes of smoke."

"What does it smell like when it changes texture like that?" she prodded.

"It never really has a smell. Just like… air I guess."

"Fresh air or air that's been circulated in the same enclosed space for too long?"

"Neither. Just… air. Like it's really crisp but there's nothing like trees or grass or flowers to it."

"Ozone?" she suggested.

"Maybe." I shrugged. "I don't go around smelling

things to commit them to memory."

"Setting that aside for the moment, how does it feel when it changes from one to the other?"

"It doesn't. It's either one or the other."

"And you're sure about that? Have you tried to summon it and let it change form?"

I ducked my head, avoiding her eye. "No."

She let out a groan. "I thought I told you to practise."

"I know, I know. And I keep meaning to but every time it comes out, I feel like I'm not in control."

"And that is the entire point of the class, Norah. To get you to learn to control it. Magic is just an extension of you. You are its master, not the other way around."

"That's easy for you to say. You're an instructor. You've done this for ages."

"Not everything comes easily to everyone. I had to fight hard to get where I am. Magic may be innate in our blood, but no two people are the same. Not everyone can so easily access and harness those gifts."

I studied her. I hadn't considered that she had struggled to learn her skills. She seemed to display them so effortlessly in class. They all did, and it felt like I was the only one who struggled. But maybe I wasn't, and the others were just better at hiding it. Or not. It wasn't like I'd really been paying attention, I'd been too caught up in my own private—and not so private—drama. But if other people struggled, and still got control of their magic, then there was some hope for me. I had to believe that.

"I can try now," I offered.

"Good. And remember, you aren't alone. I'm here to help."

I took a moment to loosen my body up and let my mind relax. I'd realised pretty fast that her warmup exercises did in fact have a purpose. As I bent over with my arms swaying in front of me, I heard Glover's voice offering instruction.

"When you stand up, visualise the shadows wrapping themselves around your hands like silk."

I stood, feeling my spine straighten one bit at a time. I exhaled and opened my eyes to find disappointment waiting for me. There was no shadow on my fingers or anywhere else in the vicinity.

"I was trying, I swear I was." I said, balling my hands into fists.

"Try it again, then. Much of magic is using our minds to manifest what we want to happen physically." She reached out and cupped my hands together. "Try letting it just pool in your hands."

I tried to picture the shadows like silky serpents, wriggling in my cupped palms. And still, nothing happened. Frustration mounted. I knew that I could make it work. I'd done it before. But all of those times had been accidental. I'd never, not a single time, despite all the extra tuition, made it happen deliberately, the way everyone else ran about doing at the blink of an eye.

"It's not working," I said and threw my arms out to the sides. Irritation laced my tone as self-doubt crept in. I shouldn't have been surprised. I was such an idiot thinking I'd suddenly get control just because I wanted to. There was a reason I'd never measured up to Micah. I couldn't make this power obey me any more than I could sprout wings and fly away from this whole annoying academy.

"You were saying," Glover said, nodding at my outstretched hands.

I looked down to see my hands cloaked in thick smoky shadows. I slowly closed and opened my hands, but the smoke remained.

"What emotion are you feeling?" Glover prodded.

"Anger. Irritation. Frustration," I replied.

"And when you manifested before, were you feeling similar emotions?"

I thought back to the fight with Celine, and Bevan's office. On Halloween. It seemed ages ago, but I didn't think those memories would be fading any time soon. I had definitely not been in a good headspace either time. "I think so."

"That may be a key piece to your puzzle, Norah. If

you've never manifested your power when you've been feeling positive emotions, it is going to be more difficult to conjure it on command."

Just what I didn't want to hear right before our extra lessons were meant to end. Even with a special ability, I was still turning out to be rubbish at magic. That little voice of self-doubt danced around in the back of my head, calling me a "loser" and a "failure" and I fought to tamp it down. I could see the tendrils of shadow winding across my fingers now, itching to be put to some purpose.

"What's the point of me learning to use it if I'm never going to be able to control it?" I spat. The shadows rose higher, dancing like the afterimages of flames looking to lick and bite and burn.

"Because you can control it." Glover slid off the desk and moved to take my hands. I wanted to pull away from her touch. I didn't want to hurt her.

To my amazement, the shadows continued to dance in my hands but left her alone. "How are you doing that?" I croaked.

She shook her head, pointing at me. "You're doing that. Your magic may be ignited by negative emotions, but you have the power to determine what happens once it's here. I suspect you had no intent to harm me just now."

"It's a fluke," I said.

She shook her head again. "No. You're more in control than you believe."

I couldn't fight the eye roll. "If I'm so in control, then why can't I make it go away?"

She clucked her tongue at me. "I didn't say you'd mastered it." After a breath she continued, "How have you managed to get it to recede before?"

"I've always had help," I mumbled, embarrassment turning my cheeks bright pink.

"That's what I'm here for," Glover said, and lightly grasped my wrists in her hands. "Needing help isn't anything to be ashamed of—both in my lecture room, and out of it."

I tried to focus on the feeling of her hands against my skin and let that ground me. Then I took a deep breath and pictured the shadows receding into my pores, willing them back to a ripple beneath the surface of my skin.

"Good." Glover's voice pulled me out of my inward contemplation. I looked down to see nothing winding and weaving between my fingers or pluming like smoke from my palms. "Keep practicing and you'll get there, Norah. It just takes time and patience."

"I'm still behind everyone else."

She flashed a knowing smile. "Then it's a good thing unique magics is a pass or fail course and I have broad liberties to determine who makes the grade."

I gave a feeble smile as I gathered my bag and left the lecture room. I knew she was trying to be encouraging in her own way. But it didn't help that no matter how much positivity she tried to buoy me with, I was still facing an uncertain future. Worse still, I had to endure two weeks at home with my parents.

"Cheer up, you'll get through it," Eva said an hour later, as we dragged our bags down to the entryway to be escorted off campus by the druids.

"You haven't met my parents," I sighed. I hadn't spoken to them in months. Not since before Micah's trial.

Across the way, I spotted Celine and her groupies casting furtive glances my way. Let them stare. At least they'd laid off me since our Halloween interaction. A chilly gust of air whipped in through the open doors and I shivered, not ready to face what that icy blast promised.

"You have someone to escort you off grounds?" Zachary's voice floated to me from my right.

"Nope," I replied, without turning to address him. "And why does it matter to you?"

He stepped up close. "Because I figure you don't want everyone knowing about your weak stomach," he whispered in my ear and grabbed my wrist to lead me out into the wintery unknown.

* * *

Spending New Year's at a maximum-security prison was

not my idea of fun. But my parents had refused to let me skip out on visiting Micah. So, instead of hiding in my bedroom practicing what little magic I had, I was standing at the locked entry to my brother's temporary prison cell. Temporary—because no-one was allowed in Daoradh unless they were a prisoner or an enforcer. Not even to visit. Its location was a closely guarded secret, and not one they'd be sharing with the family of a known traitor.

Instead, they'd transported him to another prison for a brief visit. Some sort of reward for good behaviour. It was the only one he'd be allowed all year.

"You didn't have to come," Micah's voice was dull, uninterested.

"We're worried about you, sweetheart," my mother said, trying to reach for him through the bars.

A burly guard stepped forward with a metal baton in hand, ready to swat her away if she so much as sneezed funny. With his powers bound, at least Micah didn't have to wear those awful power-suppressing cuffs. I scratched at my hands subconsciously.

"I was surprised to see you there on my big day, sis," he said, addressing me for the first time.

"You're family, Mic. Of course I'd show. Doesn't mean I think what they did was right," I said, keeping my distance.

"At least I'm alive, right? Could be worse."

159

"Don't say that," Mum said, her voice high-pitched and whiny.

"Come now, Mum, if a bloke can't joke about the next three decades of his life, how's he supposed to stay sane?"

"You didn't deserve this," I murmured.

He gave me a sullen look. "Neither do you, Nor. Neither do you." He beckoned me closer and I could almost swear my feet moved of my own accord until I stood as close as the guard seemed comfortable. "You been watching your back?"

"No one cares about me," I said.

"Don't be so sure about that. You're more valuable than you give yourself credit for. Time to let people know that."

"Time's up," the guard barked, and ushered us out of the prison.

By the time I made it back to Braeseth grounds three days later, I was in a foul mood. I didn't want to stand out. That was the exact opposite of what I'd set out to do. I wanted to fly under the radar. Not be the centre of attention. And yet, I couldn't shake the feeling that Micah knew something I didn't. Maybe they hadn't bound all of his powers after all, because I could still hear his voice in my head, egging me on as I dragged my case up to the girls' dorm.

"Need help?" a female druid enforcer called up ahead of me.

"Sure, thanks," I said.

She spotted me and her friendly demeanour changed. She marched up to me and bent down, putting her full weight on the case so there was no way I could move it. "Oh, never mind. I don't help traitors like you. Dirty misfit."

I straightened. "Excuse me?"

"You heard me. The whole lot of you are nothing but troublemakers. I've got my eye on you. If you so much as put a toe out of line, I'm going to know about it."

"What is your problem?" I snapped. "I didn't do anything to you or anyone else at this academy."

"Apples don't fall far from the tree," she said. "And I heard about your little trip on New Year's Day."

"What do I have to do to prove to you people that I am not my brother?" I snapped.

The edges of my vision grew grey and hazy, and my skin burned. Heat rippled along my exposed forearms and shadows ignited, pluming high and choking. They leapt out at the enforcer, tightening around her wrists, her throat.

"Norah!" Zachary's voice cut through the haze just enough for me to come back to myself. Shit. What the hell was I doing?

Taking ragged breaths, I forced the magic back inside me. It fought me every inch of the way, leaving every nerve ending hypersensitive. When Zachary tried to reach for my arm, I pulled away. Even the lightest pressure sent agony lancing through my elbow and down into my wrist.

"You little bitch," the female enforcer snarled, raising a hand toward me.

"Seneca, stand down," Zachary said, putting himself between us.

"Get out of the way," Seneca hissed.

"I outrank you. Stand down." The edge of authority in his tone made me stand at attention.

I hadn't paid attention to the hierarchy among our supposed protectors. I should have assumed that Zachary had a higher rank than the others. He seemed to come and go as he pleased and got the choice assignments off grounds.

"I'm reporting her. That was a direct attack," Seneca replied, arms crossed over her chest.

"She started it," I ground out in true petty fashion.

"Do what you have to do," Zachary answered, and stepped aside. He glanced at me and patted my case. "This will be waiting in your room when you're done."

I couldn't even muster a 'thanks' as I trailed Seneca to Dean Bevan's office. I was surprised to see the man sitting there behind the desk, like he'd been expecting this little display.

"What's happened?" he eyed me warily.

"She attacked me," Seneca began.

"I didn't mean to. I still can't control my power. But she accused me of being a criminal just because of my family and that's not fair," I rambled.

Bevan held up a hand to shut me up. "Miss Sheehan, while I can sympathise with your situation and I understand that you are still mastering your abilities, the druids are our guests on campus and are doing us a service by removing the curses still lingering. Please apologise and remember that any further instances may result in disciplinary action."

I stared at him, mouth agape. Had he just told me to apologise and threatened disciplinary action if I chose to defend myself against baseless accusations? I stared at him, waiting for him to say something else. To make sense. He just sat there, waiting in silence. I wasn't going to get anything more from him. What a bloody coward. He shouldn't be so concerned with making the damned druids happy. We were the pupils in his care. Shouldn't we be his top priority?

I grit my teeth, turned to Seneca, and said, "Sorry. Won't happen again."

"It better not," she answered coolly. The threat in her tone was clear. She would be watching me.

I left Bevan's office determined not to give her a chance to screw me over again. One thing was for sure: Micah had been right.

I needed to watch my back.

Chapter Fourteen

Having my Saturday mornings back felt strange. Despite not having to be anywhere, my body still woke me up at seven thirty. I rolled over and stared at Eva's sleeping form. She'd come back from the break a day late but hadn't wanted to say anything about why.

"You awake?" I whispered.

She gave a loud snore. Having shared the same space for the last four months, I knew even when she had a clogged head she didn't snore like that. She was awake.

"Very funny," I said and rolled into a sitting position, prepared to chuck a pillow at her.

"It's early, Nor. On a Saturday," she mumbled into her pillow.

"You've been getting up early with me all semester," I reminded her. "You're the morning person, remember?"

"I'm just tired." She sighed, but rolled to look at me.

I could see bags under eyes that weren't normally there. "What's going on? You've been off since break."

She exhaled slowly and turned her gaze to the ceiling. "Mum told me over Christmas that she's been trying to find my dad."

"Isn't that a good thing? You wanted to know about him for a while."

"I know, but after what happened when my powers

manifested, I kind of gave up. And it's just been the two of us for so long, I don't know, it sounds stupid and selfish but like, it was my thing."

I crawled out from beneath my blankets and crossed the room to perch on the end of her bed. "This is a whole new world for her, too. She's trying to make sense of it however she can. And she knew you wanted answers. And I mean, you are a human lie detector."

"Shut up," she said with a small smirk.

"Can't beat how I spent my holiday," I said.

"Really?" She arched a dark brow as if daring me to top her story.

"Spent New Year's in prison visiting my brother."

She flopped back against her pillow. "Yeah, you win," she said, her voice bitter. "Should have realised brother in prison trumps shady potential bio dad every time."

My heart sank. I hadn't meant to make her feel bad, and I definitely hadn't meant to minimise what she'd gone through. I really was shit in the morning.

"I didn't mean it like that," I said, knowing my words carried little weight.

She fixed me with an annoyed look. "I know you didn't. But it's still irritating that it feels like no matter what anyone else does or is going through in your orbit, you've got this automatic trump card just because of what your brother did."

"I really wish people would stop reminding me of what he's done. I know what he did. I know what he's going through now is because of the decisions he made." Massaging my temples, I tried to keep the anger in check. "I don't need my only friend giving me a hard time about it. Not when the bloody druids think I'm a ticking time bomb and Bevan seems happy to bow to their superiority."

"What are you talking about? What did the druids do?" She sat up straight, the annoyance replaced by genuine concern, not even calling me on the fact I'd been the one to bring Micah up first.

"It was stupid. This one enforcer, Seneca I guess her name is, just went off on me when all I needed was a hand getting my case up here. Telling me I was a criminal and no better than the rest of my family. That she'd be watching me. Dragged me into Bevan's office and he flat out told me to apologise for defending myself."

"That isn't fair," she said, falling right back into the supportive best friend role.

"And honestly, I've never even said two words to her before yesterday. So I don't know what crawled up her arse and died."

Eva snickered at my words, and it caught. Before long, we were both doubled over laughing. When I sat up, I felt much of the dark cloud that had hung over me overnight lifting. Maybe I should just try to put the whole Seneca debacle behind me and focus on trying to not suck in all of my classes.

"So, you've finished tutoring with Glover?" Eva asked as we headed to the kitchen for breakfast.

"Yeah. We sort of figured out that my powers are triggered when I'm angry. Not that it helps a lot," I said as I reached for a mug and the nearest pot of coffee. The nutty aroma of the steam told me it was hazelnut, and I set it back on the heating element—a tiny, flattened sphere of fire magic. I leaned in to sniff the next pot, satisfied it was normal coffee before filling my mug.

"I wouldn't say it isn't useful. You know how to trigger it. That's a step in the right direction."

"Yeah, but you've been able to control your ability for months now. I'm pathetic next to the rest of you."

"You are not pathetic, Norah. I keep telling you, not everyone is good with school and classes and everything. Maybe we just need to find the way that you learn best."

"Not at all," I muttered.

Eva just shook her head and headed for a table. By the time I joined her, she was stabbing the remnants of a crepe with her fork. She seemed determined to spear each and every crumb.

"So, I think you're right about Zachary after all," I said, hoping a change of subject would rouse her from terrorising her breakfast.

"How so?"

"Well, I mean, besides showing up to diffuse things with Seneca yesterday, he personally escorted me off grounds because he knows my stomach doesn't exactly agree with the transportation stone."

"He's looking out for you. That's sweet. You should say thank you," she said, looking up from her plate and batting her lashes at me.

"And how would you suggest I do that?" I countered.

"With your mouth." The 'duh, moron' was implied.

"I can't just go up to him and say 'Gee, thanks for deciding I'm worth your time and effort'. Besides, I don't even know if I like him that way."

"The fact you're obsessing over what you can or can't say to him tells me you do like him."

I slumped back in my seat and stared at the dark swirling contents of my mug. If her assessment was accurate—and I hated to admit that it was—how did I feel about that? I knew it wasn't fair to lump all druids together and blame them all for the actions of a select few. And he'd done nothing to make me think he thought he was better than the rest of us. Not like Seneca or the Council. But I couldn't just ignore the fact that he was an enforcer and, like it or not, he held power over me.

"It would never work, so why even bother trying?"

"Nor, don't sabotage yourself before you even give it a try. You never know. He might be the world's best kisser. Do you really want to miss out on that possibility?"

I averted my gaze, trying to keep the mental images that sprang into my mind's eye at bay. I didn't need to be thinking about kissing him. Or doing anything else with him.

"I'll think about it," I answered into my mug.

We finished eating in silence, and Eva retreated to the dorms to grab some books and find a quiet corner of the library to do her botany assignment. I should probably join her. I'd neglected that class, too. But really, how much interest could one person show in boring old plants? It wasn't like I was ever going to be a healer or whatever. Not wanting to be out in the chilly January air but refusing to stay cooped up in the dorms, I wound my way through the academy's corridors. I wasn't sure what I was expecting to find, but I certainly didn't anticipate Celine and her lackeys clustered together at the end of the hall. I darted into the open door to the potions laboratory and prayed they hadn't spotted me. I wasn't in the mood to deal with whatever drama she was cooking up.

"Odd place for you to be this early in the morning," a voice called from behind me.

I whirled to find Rathbone sitting across the room

with a dog-eared book in his lap.

"Odd place for an instructor who doesn't teach this subject to be, too," I countered.

He smiled and set his book aside. Today he wore his hair in a loose tail at the nape of his neck. The scruff on his chin was more pronounced and I could see the hint of dark circles under his eyes.

"Whilst I'd be thrilled to think one of my students is taking their studies seriously, would it be fair to assume you're hiding out in here for a reason?" he probed.

"Maybe." I didn't need him getting involved in the drama with Celine. I didn't need everyone else trying to fight my battles for me.

"If I'm honest, I am, too," he said, leaning forward and lowering his voice.

Don't engage.

"What are you hiding from?" The words leapt past my lips before I could think better of them.

"Let's just say I needed some space from our enforcer guests. They can be a little chafing with their perimeter sweeps and such."

I gaped at Rathbone. He didn't like or trust the enforcers either? But surely he could spend time in his own lecture room or wherever else the instructors gathered on campus?

"They are kind of annoying," I said.

"Not to pry, but how have you been doing, Norah? Much as I'd like to think you not taking me up on my offer to talk was because you were settling in better, I suspect that might be wishful thinking on my behalf."

"I'm fine, really. School just isn't my thing," I said, shoving my hands into my pockets.

"I can understand that," he said.

"Yeah, sure."

"It pains me to remind you that I, too, was once a teenager going through my own magical education. I remember how difficult it could be. Now, I know I'm just your energy manipulations instructor but if you need help in other subjects, I'm happy to share what I know." He paused and chuckled. "Well, maybe not botany. I'm pretty terrible with plants."

"I appreciate the offer, I do, but I'll be fine. I'm getting better with conjuring energy. I'll be doing it with both hands before you know it."

"I know you will. It's all about mastering your own mind. Once you're the one in control, you can do anything."

"Thanks, Instructor." I peered back out into the corridor. Celine and her cronies were gone. "Not that I don't appreciate you baring your soul and whatever, but I think I'm done hiding."

He gestured toward the door, as if giving me

permission to leave. "Just don't tell the enforcers I'm in here, all right?"

I mimed sealing my lips and tossing the key. He picked up his book and turned his attention back to it. Stepping out of the potions lab, I realised I still had no idea what I was looking to do with the day. Idleness never ended well for me.

* * *

By Monday morning, I'd wrestled my idleness into something semi-productive. Even if I wasn't having extra lessons with Glover, I could still practise some of the techniques she'd given me. And I'd even seen some results. But, as I sat in Magical Law, I caught sight of an enforcer uniform through the doorway. I leaned forward to catch sight of a face and recoiled when Seneca's gaze met mine. She glared at me and positioned herself so that she could watch me for the rest of the lesson.

"I need to run back to the dorm. I forgot my notes for Cultural Studies. I'll meet you there," Eva said, bolting from the room the moment our lesson ended, before I even had a chance to stand up or respond.

Having no particular desire to go to class myself, I took my time packing up. Out of the corner of my eye, I saw Celine lingering by her desk until it was just us and her two besties left in the room. Great. What did she want now? She gestured to Miranda, who shuffled across the room and stationed herself at the door. I had enough of a view to see that Seneca had abandoned her post spying on me.

"Heard you can't keep from getting into it with those arsehole druids," Celine said with a sugary smile.

"What business is it of yours who I get involved with?" I answered without making eye contact.

"Oh, come on, Norah. You can't possibly think they are here for our protection and to help us. They treat us like we're dirt."

Much as I hated to admit it, she had a point. I shrugged. "Maybe. I still don't see why you care about what happens to me or why I should care about whatever it is you are doing."

Celine cast a glance at Miranda, who nodded. "Because we're going to do something about it. I know you keep saying I don't know your brother and maybe you're right. But he wasn't wrong wanting to fight for those of us who are at the bottom. Even if some of us are higher up in that chain than others."

"You really think three first year students can do something to change things around here?" I demanded.

Celine crossed her arms over her chest and gave me a haughty look. Beside her, Jessa said, "It's not just three of us."

Interesting.

174

"It could be four, if you've got the balls to actually do something about all the shit you've been dealt with," Celine said.

The way she balled her hands into tight fists and turned her back on Jessa suggested her lackey had said more than she was supposed to. That was fine, they didn't trust me. I didn't particularly trust them, either.

But again, she had a point. The druids had ruined my brother's life when they could have been lenient. When they could have found a way to help him, rather than just lock him away. And they'd ignored my requests over summer. Sure, I was kind of grateful they'd said no, but it seemed stupid they had that much say over the rest of us. Especially when they didn't see us as equals. We all had magic, what made them so bloody special? The image of Seneca watching me during class flashed into my brain followed by the horrible way she'd talked to me when semester began. She'd had no right. She wasn't better than me, just because she'd been born a druid and I hadn't. Just because I channelled energy and not elements. I deserved better. *We* deserved better. The telltale haze at the edges of my vision and warm tingling in my fingers foreshadowed the magic about to pop up unbidden.

Celine gave me a knowing smirk. She'd sensed what was coming and wasn't afraid anymore. If she was looking to recruit me, she saw a purpose for me.

Balling my hands into fists to keep my anger in check, I said, "You know what, you have a point. They could use taking down a peg or two."

I sucked in a breath and nodded.

"Whatever it is, I'm in."

Chapter Fifteen

Not surprisingly, Celine was keeping mum on her big plan. All she would tell me was that it was going to change everything, and we wouldn't have to be stuck under the thumb of the druids for much longer. I'd insisted that we should do whatever it was now and be rid of them, but she'd been firm. Whatever it was, it had to wait.

Keeping the truth from Eva hurt. I knew that she shared some of the same concerns about the druids, at least as it related to criminal justice, but wanting people to be treated fairly was a far cry from revolution. I didn't want to think that whatever we were doing was that impactful but the fervour that Celine displayed all but promised big waves. Besides, Celine had also made it clear that her little invitation was for me and me alone. Even if I'd wanted to bring Eva in on the plan, it wasn't allowed. I had no doubt Celine would disavow me if I tried to change things behind her back.

Knowing that Eva could pick up on any lie I told, I had to be more guarded around her than was comfortable. She didn't say anything all through January and into February, but the way she kept glancing at me during our energy manipulation study session right before Valentine's Day got to me.

"What?" I sighed.

"What do you mean, what?" she replied over the top of her notebook.

"You keep looking at me and it's starting to creep me out," I answered.

"You've been weird lately. Quieter than usual. What's up?"

That forced silence had been my shield against her ability for this long, but such a direct confrontation couldn't be ignored. She wouldn't let it go and I knew the minute I started talking, she'd smell the lies wafting off me like cheap perfume.

"Can't a girl be contemplative?" I murmured.

"Not you. I know you want people not to pay attention to you, but that rule doesn't apply to your best friend. You're going through something and I want to help." She set her notes aside and scooted over to sit on the edge of my bed.

"I've just been thinking about how crappy the druids have been treating my family, I guess." That was technically true.

"I know it's been hard, but like you've been saying, you aren't defined by his actions. You are your own person."

"I'm finding it harder to figure out who that is than I expected."

"I have something that could take your mind off of things," she said with a sly grin.

"No."

"I haven't even said anything," she protested.

"I know that look. You're planning something social. Don't you remember the last time we tried to do something social? Shadows erupted from my hands."

"Well, it's not like you can manifest your powers for the first time more than once. Besides, you've barely talked about a certain enforcer since the start of semester. Weren't you going to think about giving it a go?"

Come to think of it, I hadn't seen Zachary around the grounds since the end of last semester. Maybe his assignment had been changed, or maybe he'd just realised what a loser I was and made the smart decision to distance himself from me.

"Trying to tread water and catch up on lessons has made romance take a back seat."

"What better time than Valentine's to put it in the forefront? There's a sanctioned party happening tomorrow night. You know they'll have enforcer chaperones to make sure things don't get too out of hand."

"If I agreed to go, and that's a huge if, what makes you think he'd be there and want to spend time with me instead of doing his job?"

She chewed her lower lip and gave let out a giddy giggle. "I may have checked the roster of who is chaperoning and he's not on it."

"Okay, so he's not going to be working. But what makes you think he'd still show up to the party?"

Her voice turned breathy. "I may also have mentioned to him that you might be there and you wanted to thank him properly for his help with everything."

I thumped her in the arm. "You did not."

"One of us deserves a little love."

"Why can't that someone be you?" I whined.

"Because no one here interests me."

"I'm not going to have a choice in the matter, am I?"

"Not even a little."

I let out a huff. "Fine, but you better do my make-up and hair like last time. If I'm going to show up to this party, I'd better look flipping amazing."

* * *

"These jeans feel ridiculous," I complained as I tugged at the unnaturally tight fit of the jeans. They were exactly my size, but were clearly meant for someone who preferred to be painted into their clothing.

"Stop complaining. You look great," Eva hissed, and swatted at my hand.

We headed for the auditorium. Apparently,

administration-sanctioned revelry meant being in a single room with only limited entry and exit points. And no places to hide and make out…or anything else. Somehow the seats had been removed, and the sloping floor led down to an elaborate dance floor. A table pressed up against one wall featured snacks and drinks. I intended to stay clear of those. I didn't trust my classmates not to spike whatever had been provided.

"I don't see him," I said, crossing my arms over my chest. It only served to accentuate my chest in the ribbed burnt orange top I wore.

"You're not looking very hard," she commented, lifting her hand to point to the opposite corner while biting into something that smelled vaguely of cinnamon.

I followed the trajectory of her hand and spotted Zachary lurking in the corner. He was out of uniform and instead wore a button down dark blue dress shirt and black fitted trousers. He looked so normal and very much the attractive older guy who should be off limits.

"Go talk to him," Eva ordered with a shove reminiscent of a mother bird kicking her babies out of the nest to test their wings.

I moved around the edge of the room, letting my gaze slide over the other students present. Some were from the older years. They were vaguely recognisable faces but nothing more. I spotted some of the students in my own year. Celine held court at the far edge of the dance floor with a flock of girls around her, preening and hanging on her every word. Rory stood with his arm draped over her shoulders, drinking from a glass. He wasn't paying attention to her, more like using her as an armrest. *Douchebag.*

When I finally made it to where Zachary stood, I'd lost all sense of how words worked. He spotted me and closed the distance between us.

"Glad you made it without any problems this time," he said over the sudden pulse of music.

"Yeah, uh, me, too," I said lamely.

"That colour looks nice on you," he said before hanging his head. "Sorry, I'm a bit rubbish at this."

That admission brought down my own nerve-fuelled walls. "Glad I'm not the only one."

"You want to go somewhere quieter?" he offered and pointed to the door not far away.

Knowing my classmates, leaving with an enforcer would raise eyebrows and would make the rumour mill rounds. Celine would no doubt question it and my loyalty to her still-vague plan. But I could deal with her. I'd just say I was keeping tabs on the enforcers and what they were doing. I gestured to let him lead me out.

The moment we were in the entryway and the doors closed, I exhaled. The music which had been a pounding bass had been giving me a headache I hadn't realised was there until the sound was gone. I rubbed at my temple until the throbbing dissipated.

"You haven't been around much lately," I noted as he led me to an alcove down the hall that led to the library and stairwell to the lecture room.

"I've been around, just busy," he replied. He had to know his response sounded cagey. "I haven't been avoiding you or anything like that."

"Good, because a girl could wonder if I did something to horribly offend you."

"Well, I mean, you did nearly choke out one of my colleagues."

I noted his choice of words. He didn't say friends. "Let's not talk about her."

"Fair enough." He leaned in. "Though between you and me, she deserved it."

"Thanks." I smiled. "I mean it. For everything you've done. And I swear I'll get my stomach under control sometime."

"I like getting to take you places."

I'm pretty sure my cheeks flamed the same colour as my shirt just then. "Highlight of your day, I'm sure."

"At least I generally get decent food out of it," he said with a smile tugging at the corners of his mouth in a way that made my heart squeeze.

We hadn't told anyone that on the trip back to my parents' for Christmas break he'd stopped and bought me ice cream to help calm my stomach. That was two semi-dates we'd had now. But who was counting? "And you're always the gentleman and pay."

"My mum raised me right," he said with a nod.

As we sat there in the semi-darkness, I realised I knew nothing about him. Not the important things. Not the things a girl should know if she had any chance of ending the night kissing him. "How long ago did you graduate from… Um, what's the enforcer academy actually called?" That was probably the least romantic question I could have asked.

"Krakenvale. I finished training two years ago."

"What made you want to do it?"

"I guess it's what people expect, you know? You go to an academy and people see what you're good at and they put on you on a track."

"So, someone else said, 'you'd be a banging enforcer' and that was the end of it?"

He tilted his head to one side. "I suppose so. I didn't really question it. I was too busy working hard to make the grade. Krakenvale's standards are…exacting."

"But, like, when you were little, what did you want to do?"

"I wanted to help people. My mum doesn't have any

magic. She's a general practice doctor. Treats all sorts of people. I used to love going to the clinic with her."

"Couldn't you have been a healer or something then?"

"I'm helping people this way, too. Just not quite how I thought originally." He looked at me, his gaze so intense I thought he might be trying to read my mind. "What about you? What do you want to do when this is all over?"

"That assumes I make it through to graduation."

"Okay, hypothetically, having graduated successfully, what do you want to do?"

"I don't know. I've never been one of those people who had a passion for a particular thing. I spent most of my childhood chasing Micah's shadow, only to realise I was never going to be as good as him at well… anything. I spent all that time so focused on him, I never stopped to think about me."

No one else had taken much of an interest, either. My parents barely acknowledged my presence over summer or break. Their attention had still been laser-focused on Micah.

"I suppose if I could be anything, maybe I'd like to own a shop or something. I don't know. It seems silly."

"What would you sell in this shop of yours?" he asked, propping his chin on his hand.

"I can make a decent pot of coffee," I replied.

"I see, you're going to run a coffee shop, then. That artisanal coffee with the little art in it?"

"Hell, no. It's meant to be drunk, not set up in an art museum."

He snorted with laughter, presumably at the indignant expression I could feel on my face, and then he grew serious again.

"Well, you'll have your first paying customer on opening day. Because, I, too, agree that coffee is meant to be drunk as it is."

"Maybe it could share space with your clinic when you decide to actually go into medicine," I replied.

"That sounds nice," he said. His hand hovered over mine and I caught it twitch, like he wanted to take mine but was too afraid of it.

"I'm crazy, aren't I? Thinking about all this." I sighed.

"Not at all. It's good to have dreams. It makes the monotony of real life more bearable. And for what it's worth, you'd make an excellent café owner, magic or no."

"Thanks." The closeness of his body to mine sent shivers down my spine. "This is going to sound so stupid but, I'm not imagining this. There's something here. Between us."

My throat went dry as I waited for him to deny it.

He pursed his lips. "You're not imagining things."

"And am I right in thinking that right now, you really want to do something about it?"

His cheeks flushed red and his smile faltered. He dragged his hand back from mine, putting more distance between us. "It wouldn't be appropriate."

"Screw appropriate," I said and stood, putting myself in his path. If he wanted to get past me, he was going to have to make physical contact.

"It's just not a good time, Norah. If things were different, then maybe, but I have a job to do and there's a power dynamic whether we like it or not…"

Oh, shut up.

I leaned in, slapped both of my palms on his cheeks and kissed him on the mouth.

Chapter Sixteen

The kiss ended faster than it started. I came to my senses and stepped back to give him a wide berth if he wanted to bolt past me and never speak to me again. Instead, he stood there looking dazed.

"I'm an idiot," I said, trying to cover the awkwardness blossoming between us.

"Not the word I'd use," he replied, touching the tip of his finger to his lips.

I wanted to apologise over and over until he forgave me—and possibly agreed to pretend it never happened—but there was no time before a bloodcurdling scream issued from the corridor to our right. We both took off running, and it only took a few strides before Zachary outpaced me. He skidded around the corner and stopped, throwing out an arm to bar my way. The dazed expression had been replaced by something far more serious. He tilted his head to the side, as if trying to find the origin of the scream.

Without a word, he made for the stairwell. We were halfway to the next floor when another scream went up. It was louder, more pained this time. That only spurred Zachary onward. He slammed his shoulder through the door at the top of the stairs. On the floor where students weren't supposed to be because it had been cursed. My mouth went dry and I couldn't speak to warn Zachary to be careful. To ask what was going on.

He pressed himself to the wall just beyond the open door and pressed a finger to his lips to ensure I understood that silence was key. I tried to mirror his posture and crammed myself against the opposite side of the door.

"How'd you know it came from three floors up?" I hissed after what seemed an eternity.

"I could feel the sound vibrations."

"Right. Of course, that makes perfect sense," I whispered.

"Air is my element. And that includes tracing the origin point of sounds. Kind of a big deal," he answered.

I considered his words for a moment. Having air-based magic made a lot of things click into place. How he'd heard Eva and my conversation the day we met. Why he seemed so comfortable transporting through the air. Probably how he hauled my case upstairs.

"I'm not disputing that is a pretty sweet power, but how exactly does that help us with the screaming?"

He looked at me and for the first time, it was like he saw me for the eighteen-year-old untrained and unclassified witch I was. Like I was a child he had to protect and defend. Some girls might have found that charming or heroic even. Their knight in shining armour.

I felt patronised. Just because I didn't have the skills he did, it didn't mean I couldn't take care of myself.

"There's no us here, Norah. Just me. I need you to stay here and be quiet. I'll handle this."

"That's a bit presumptuous, don't you think? You don't even know what's going on," I snapped, my irritation bubbling to the surface.

"This is literally why I'm here, Norah." He broke off from his harsh whisper and snapped a glance down the corridor, and then back to me. "If someone's up here who shouldn't be and the latent magic's gone off, then it's my job to deal with this."

He didn't give me time to come back with a witty retort. He slunk off down the corridor and the way his hair ruffled around him despite there being no breeze told me he was summoning his power. I didn't want to sit here and wait for him to get hurt. I waited until the count of ten and then hurried after him.

"Calm down," Zachary's voice called up ahead.

"I am calm," an annoyingly familiar voice replied.

I crept up to the corner and peered around in time to see Seneca standing in the middle of the corridor with her shirt in flames. Her hands were glowing red balls of living fire. Another enforcer stood beside her, looking like he'd come out of a lake. His clothes were so waterlogged I could see them weighing him down.

"You need to get control," Zachary chided.

"It hurts," Seneca said, her voice pitching into a whine.

The slight ruffling of Zachary's hair stopped, and he took a noticeable step back. "Tell me what happened."

"We were checking for any last remnants of the cube. We thought this part had been cleared but it hit us before we realised it," water guy answered.

"That doesn't make sense," Zachary said. "I cleared this area myself."

I couldn't see his face, but I could picture his brow furrowing with determination. The flames in Seneca's hands leapt higher, catching a bit of fabric on her collar that hadn't ignited yet. I also had no idea what cube they were talking about. I couldn't see anything in their immediate vicinity that would have triggered their magic to go haywire.

"Well, you clearly missed something," Seneca snapped.

Zachary started to pace and his footsteps echoed loudly in my ears. I didn't know what he planned to do, but I was eager to see him sort it out. He spun a quarter turn and said, "I know you didn't listen to me. You might as come out."

I shuffled into view and the look on Seneca's face went from pain to pissed off. I stayed behind Zachary. I didn't know how far she could lob one of those fireballs, and I wasn't keen to find out.

"What's this cube thing? Maybe if I can find it, I can stop whatever it's doing to them," I offered.

"You don't know anything, do you?" Seneca snarled.

"Getting close to whatever is causing this is only going to lead to you being in the same position. It's syphoning their magic and turning what's left inward against them like a poison," Zachary explained without taking his eyes off the others.

Had this been what Micah had done? I pushed down the conflicting emotions as I tried to focus on how to help here and now. "What can I do?"

"The salve I used on you on Halloween," Zachary said.

"Great, got any on you in those fancy trousers of yours?"

"I wasn't exactly planning on defusing magical bombs tonight," he answered.

"So that's a no, then. Any other ideas?"

"It's not that hard to make," he said, crouching down.

I didn't like where this was headed. "I'm not very good with botany. You're better off getting it yourself."

"Can't leave them. You need to go to the botany lab."

"I don't even know what to get," I protested.

"You can do this, Norah. Please, go."

I bit back a groan and raced back the way we'd come. I made it to the first floor and collided with Eva. She looked tired but she had a smile on her face.

"So, did you and Zachary have a fun night?" She sounded a little tipsy.

"We kissed, but right now we've got bigger things to worry about. Come on, I need your help."

I grabbed her by the wrist and hauled her back to the lecture rooms. She didn't argue, just let me lead her to the botany lab. I skidded to a halt and stared at the rows of plants.

"What are we looking for?" Having a purpose seemed to sober my best friend right up.

"The stuff Zachary put on my hands on Halloween. He needs like a lot of it. And we don't exactly have a lot of time."

"Right. Get me the textbook. I need to double check the quantities."

And this was exactly why I'd hoped I would run into her. Eva's natural talent—and yeah, okay, the fact she actually put some effort into her studies—meant she definitely had the edge over me here. I grabbed the book sitting on the nearest desk and passed it to her.

In short order, she called out the different plants we needed, pointing some of them out when I didn't recognise them, and I clipped the leaves and buds as requested. She pulled a mortar and pestle from somewhere and began mashing the plants together into a paste.

"Can we make it airborne?" I blurted.

"Um, what?"

"It needs to cover a lot of space at once and we can't exactly get close to apply it. We need to aerosolise it."

"Um... yeah, I think so. Just give me a minute." She rubbed at her temples as I went in search of a spray bottle.

I found one used to water the plants and wrenched the top off. When I turned back, I found Eva adding the paste to some clear solution in a beaker and swirling it around.

"Is that going to do the trick?" I asked, and offered up the bottle.

"Honestly, I don't know, but it's the best we've got. Short of heating it up to make it truly a liquid and catching the vapours, I'm sort of flying blind."

It would have to do. She funnelled the brownish sludgy compound into the spray bottle and tightened the nozzle. I snatched it back from her and darted out of the lab. There was no time for creeping around and playing by the rules. I wasn't going to leave Zachary up there exposed to some sort of magical bomb.

"We can't go up there," Eva called when I started up

the last flight of stairs.

"Don't have a choice. That's where they need it." I pivoted to look down at her. "You don't have to come. The dean already thinks I'm a screw-up, no-one round here is going to be surprised that I'm breaking the rules. But that doesn't mean you need to go down with me."

"I'd be a terrible friend and roommate if I let you go up there alone." She marched up the last few steps.

The corridor was eerily silent as I led her to where I'd left the druids. I wondered if maybe Zachary was somehow using his air magic to muffle the sounds of the others. I took the last turn to find Zachary a further distance from Seneca and the other guy. They both looked worse than when I'd left.

"Do you have it?" Zachary reached out a hand to me.

"Yes, but you can't get close to them, remember?" I answered, keeping a tight grip on the bottle.

"I can't believe you're trusting a misfit to save us," Seneca seethed.

"This misfit may be the only thing that stops your own magic from rotting you from the inside out," I snarled.

"Why am I not surprised that you know exactly how it works?" she demanded. I opened my mouth to reply but ended up just shaking my head. I'd been guessing, but that sounded pretty horrific. Had Micah really been a part of that?

"I'd ask what the hell is going on, but now is clearly not the time for questions," Eva said, and stepped back.

Zachary eyed my spray bottle. I took a deep breath and swallowed my fear. I could do this.

"I need you to trust me," I said. "And um, provide a little direction."

"Tell me what you need."

"I think we've got it to a consistency where we can spray it, but since this stops magic, we want it to go in the right direction. So, whatever you can do to make sure we don't get blow back would be brilliant."

He held up both of his hands and his palms glowed a cheery yellow hue. "Ready when you are."

"You can't be serious," Seneca huffed. Sweat slicked every exposed inch of skin. There was also considerably more of that skin exposed as the fire burned away the fabric, though I noticed the fire didn't burn the flesh it touched. It couldn't, if I recalled the theory correctly. Not her, at least. It could hurt anyone else who got close enough, though. Like me.

"Let her try," her watery companion said. It almost sounded like he had water in his lungs. *Was his magic drowning him from the inside?*

Pushing that morbid thought aside, I raised the bottle and aimed it at him. It wasn't that I wanted anyone to suffer, but he seemed in more danger with the water than she did with the fire. And maybe I was a little vindictive. But only a little. Here went everything. My fingers squeezed the trigger on the nozzle and the brownish goo trickled out in a dribble that hit the floor rather than anything useful.

Panic rose up in me, sending flares to my own magic, and I fought to keep it under control. I did *not* need an impromptu shadow show right now.

"It's okay," Zachary said, eyeing my hands. "You're going to be fine. Just take a deep breath."

Deep breath. Right. We didn't have time for me to lose control right now. I sucked in another breath and focused on the pair of figures down the hallway, standing almost completely immobile as they fought an inner battle against their own magic. If they could stay calm, so could I.

I nodded to Zachary.

"Okay, I'm good."

"Yes," he said, with a small smile. "You are."

"What?"

"What?"

Water guy cleared this throat.

"Uh, little help here?"

"Help. Yeah. Right," I said, nodding again, and Zachary snapped back into enforcer mode.

"Okay, squeeze it again, and keep it going," he said. "I'll take care of the rest."

He held his palm up, and it glowed yellow.

I aimed the bottle and this time when I squeezed the trigger, a fine brown mist erupted from the nozzle. Zachary's hands blazed bright as the mist whizzed toward the waterlogged druid. I kept squeezing until it looked like he wasn't going to dry drown before turning the bottle on Seneca. The effect on her was more obvious. The fireballs consuming her fists died to embers and then vanished altogether. She patted out the flames on her ankles and I barely hid the snicker at her standing there in her underwear.

"Good thinking turning it into a mist. I wouldn't have thought of that," Zachary said, and then added with a frown, "At least not in time."

The tips of my ears burned at his words. I turned to get a comforting word from my roommate, but she was nowhere to be seen. At least until she reappeared with blankets.

"I really thought I'd cleared this part, Brayden," Zachary said to the watery druid.

"Guess you're not infallible, airhead," Brayden replied with a tired smile and accepted the blanket from Eva.

"I'm reporting this to the High Enforcer," Seneca said and draped the other blanket over her body.

I wasn't sure what she had to report. Wasn't this the thing they'd supposedly been brought in to deal with?

"You two should go back to your dorm," Zachary said as Brayden and Seneca marched down the corridor out of view. He paused and then added, "You're just full of surprises today."

He headed after the other druids, and I couldn't help but feel embarrassed all over again.

"What was that about?" Eva needled as we headed for the dorm as directed.

"No idea," I replied.

She arched one dark brow at me and tapped the side of her nose. "Liar."

"I caught him off guard when I kissed him."

She threw out a hand and I lurched into her, staggering backwards as I caught my balance. "Wait, you're the one who kissed him? You left that detail out before." She smiled big. "And I thought you were being a wuss about the whole thing."

"I don't know. Maybe it was the fact it was Valentine's Day or whatever, but I just decided to hell with it and he was being kind of cute and rambling and I just… kissed him."

"Well, how was it?" She had the decency to wait to ask that question until we were behind closed doors.

"Brief. But good," I admitted.

"I can't believe you had the balls to actually kiss him. I'm proud of you."

"Thanks. He said nothing could happen and I mean, he's like a lot older than me, so maybe he's right."

She waved her hand dismissively. "Age is just a number. He's probably worried about the whole power dynamic thing."

"He did mention that." I said with a nod. We had no idea how long the druids intended to post up here at Braeseth. There was every possibility they could be gone come next year. That would give us the freedom to do whatever we pleased. Assuming I hadn't flunked out by then.

"He seemed pretty pleased with how you saved his friends."

"They aren't his friends. I mean, he didn't say they were his friends. And they didn't seem to like him much. Well, maybe that Brayden guy, but not Seneca. Whatever, it probably doesn't matter because she's going to find some way to pin what happened on me or claim I botched things just because she hates me."

"You're the reason she's not burning up inside. She should be grateful."

Somehow I doubted that woman had a grateful bone in her body. But the night's events did raise questions. If Zachary had been right and he'd defused whatever bomb had been there, who had set a new one? And why?

Chapter Seventeen

Dean Bevan never called me into his office to ask about what happened on Valentine's Day, but the enforcers doubled up security on the cursed corridors. Anyone who so much as set foot on the stairs leading up to the floor got a stern look and even a shove back the way they'd come. I'd even seen a few people trying to put chains on the door and lock them with the most complicated locks I'd ever seen. But that could have also been an April Fools prank, it was tough to say.

But it seemed like finally everyone had got the message to stay clear of the cursed corridors. I may have imagined it, but I also saw even less of Zachary over the next two months than I had since second semester began. And it wasn't for lack of trying. Every time I went to and from class, I scanned the faces of the uniformed druids roaming the halls and he just wasn't there. I knew he had a higher rank than Seneca, and probably Brayden, too, so maybe he was recalled by the council for another assignment. Or maybe he was just avoiding me like the plague.

"You're doing it again," Eva said as she sat beside me under the tree in the courtyard we'd claimed at the start of the year.

The weather had warmed as winter receded and April

showers pummelled the ground with more water than necessary at every opportunity. At least today everything had dried out, which was good, because I'd been starting to feel like an aquatic animal for a while. I looked at my friend.

"Doing what?"

"Brooding over him."

"I am not brooding. I'm just…concerned. I mean, I thought the kiss was decent. And he seemed to think so, too, but I haven't seen him in months. It's like he just turned invisible."

Come to think of it, could he use his air magic to do that? No, probably not. I'd never heard of anyone turning invisible before. Shame. Would have been a pretty cool power. Way better than murderous shadows. Pushing the thought aside, I stretched my legs out in front of me and held up my hands. I concentrated and let the magic inside me bubble to the surface. I had to make a conscious decision not to let the shadows out to play. I was determined to practise forming electricity. I'd been improving, sort of. A bit, at least. I could actually get the energy to pool in my hands and mash together into something resembling a blob. It wasn't pretty, but I didn't think Rathbone took off points for how attractive our magic came out.

"You think you botched it with him by making the

first move," Eva said, scrutinising my face. I avoided her eye and kept my attention on the splash of energy in my hands.

"I mean, most guys expect you to be the one getting kissed. It's stupid and misogynistic but that's how it is. Maybe I did scare him off."

"Or maybe he's just biding his time until the druids aren't here anymore to ask you out properly."

As if on cue, a pair of druids marched by our spot. Their gazes slid over us and I closed my hands, extinguishing the energy to make it clear I wasn't a threat. They shook their heads and moved on.

"Given what happened back in February, I doubt the druids will be gone for a while yet," I said.

Well, not unless whatever Celine was planning actually worked. She'd still been keeping quiet on details since I'd agreed to join their little band of delinquents. I honestly wasn't sure what she was waiting for, but I kept my mouth shut. I didn't want her to kick me out now that I was in it. Not least because as much as I understood her cause, I didn't trust her, either. She'd been a right bitch to me since we'd met and the fact was, I didn't like her. That wasn't about to change any time soon.

Beside me, my bag started vibrating. The reverberations were low enough I don't think Eva noticed, but they danced up my leg in an unnerving pattern. What was that? As discreetly as I could, I slid my hand into my bag and groped around inside for the offending object. My fingers finally brushed the communication stone Kelsey had given me so many months ago. I'd been neglecting getting in touch with her. She wouldn't approve of what I was doing, either.

"I need to go to the loo. I'll be back," I told my roommate and scurried to my feet.

"You okay?" Concern creased her brow, and I quickly ran my mind over my words, assessing them. They weren't technically a lie. I hadn't said I needed to *use* the toilet, just that I needed to go there. I didn't plan to stick around to find out if her powers had recognised the distinction.

"Yeah. Fine," I said, and raced toward the entryway.

I had no idea how long I had to answer the stone—or even how to do that—but I knew I didn't want to be having a conversation with a rock in view of my classmates. Most of them didn't trust me already. I found an empty alcove—the toilets were halfway across the academy—and pulled the stone out.

"Uh, hello?" I said, lifting the rock close to my mouth and feeling totally dumb. I contorted my body so that I could hide the rock from the view of passersby. I even set my bag over my legs for added protection.

"Norah! I'm so glad you answered." Kelsey's voice

emanated from the stone but had an odd underwater quality to it. Maybe that was just how it worked?

"Didn't know if I was doing it right," I replied, still holding the stone close to my lips.

"I'm guessing you've got the stone pretty close to your mouth. Would you mind moving it back a bit? It's coming in a bit like you're shouting," she said.

I was grateful she couldn't see the abashed look on my face as I nestled the stone in the little hollow between my knees. "Better?" I still didn't raise my voice.

"Much." I could hear the smile in her voice. "I hope I wasn't interrupting anything or calling during a lesson."

"Nope," I said. "Timing is good."

"Good. Well, I hadn't heard from you and I know how rough things have been, so I just wanted to check in. How are you?" There was an underlying note of anxiety in her tone.

I shrugged before realising she couldn't see it. "Getting by. Exams are coming up soon. Not sure I'm ready for them."

"You can do it. I know you can."

They were nice words and it was good to hear them—from one person, at least—but she had nothing to base them on.

"We'll see, I suppose." I said. "What about you? How've you been?"

"Oh, I've been good, thanks for asking."

Dead air filled the conversation and I wondered if I'd done something to lose the connection. As I sat there, I wanted to ask her questions about what she'd been through with Micah, but I knew it wasn't my business. We barely knew each other. She'd stood up for me with the council and given me some words of encouragement, but we weren't friends. Not in the same way as me and Eva. She didn't owe me anything.

"I appreciate you checking up on me," I said eventually. "It's nice. Not many people would have bothered."

"Have you made any friends?" She sounded almost maternal. Except my mother didn't care if I made friends or not. We'd barely spoken a word since visiting Micah. It was clear where her attention was right now, and it wasn't on her disappointment of a daughter.

I shook my head, clearing the bitterness, and focussed back on Kelsey's question.

"Yeah, a couple. My roommate is pretty amazing, actually."

"Good. I'm glad you're finding your people. It's one of the great things about the academies, you know. People from all walks of life get to meet each other, when otherwise they wouldn't."

An odd static came through the stone and the

vibrations shifted. Instead of coming out of all sides evenly, they seemed to be coming from just the right side, burrowing into my knee.

"You still there?" I whispered, leaning closer again. Maybe she couldn't hear me.

"Yes, I'm here. Look, I should let you go. I just wanted to know you were okay," she said, and the anxiety in her tone somehow leapt out of the stone and coiled around me, constricting my gut.

The stone stopped vibrating against my knees and I scooped it up, stowing it back in the bottom of my bag. While I couldn't deny I was pleasantly surprised she had bothered to check up on me, it did make me wonder; why now? She'd had just as much time to get in touch as I had. Was she feeling guilty for not initiating contact? After all, she'd been the one to give me the stone and tell me to use it. She also knew from our limited interactions that I wasn't very good with magical objects. I hadn't even known what the stones were when she showed me. I tried to ease the apprehension taking hold of me, but it refused to let go. Maybe having some time to myself in the dorm would help settle things.

I made it halfway there before electricity lashed out and bit into my wrist. I spun to find Celine on the other end of the energy.

"What the hell are you doing?" I demanded.

The energy vanished, and I resisted the urge to rub the sore and red skin of my wrist. She stepped in close. For the first time in forever, she wasn't flanked by Jessa or Miranda. I'd come to assume they were magically tethered to her like some weird symbiotes leeching off her popularity.

"I could ask you the same thing."

Grey washed out her face, turning her red hair dull and lifeless, and my palms grew warm. A tiny voice in the back of my head told me to keep my emotions in check. That this wasn't the time to unleash my power, especially with the druids doing double patrols. I was on at least two people's shit list and they'd take any excuse to haul me to the dean. And attacking Celine in a more aggressive manner than she'd used to get my attention would make her suspicious. I counted to five in my head, willing the shadows back into their place. I didn't need another confrontation.

"What are you even talking about?"

"You don't think I didn't notice you slinking off with that druid at the Valentine's Day dance?"

"Seriously? You're mad about that? Still?"

"The optics look atrocious, Norah," she answered.

I laughed. "First off, that was months ago. So, I don't see why it's important now. Second, it's really none of your business who I spend my time with."

"Did you conveniently forget what we're fighting for? Or is your libido so overpowering it just erased it from your head?"

"Look, he likes me," I said. "It's been obvious for months and he's attractive enough, I guess. I was feeding into what he wanted. I was trying to keep an eye on him, see if I could get him to trust me so when the time comes, maybe he looks the other way."

It was scary how easily the lies fell out of my mouth. And yet, I despised throwing Zachary under the bus. Thankfully Eva was nowhere near me to call me on my extreme pile of bullshit.

"So, you mean to tell me you flirted with him just to get him to trust you so you can use him later?" she repeated.

"Yes."

Her annoyed pout vanished, replaced by a wide grin. "Brilliant. I knew you'd be useful." The smile was short-lived, though. "But I heard you helped out some of those other druids that night, too."

"If I didn't act, he would have got suspicious. And don't worry, I took my sweet time. They suffered for a while before I saved them."

I could still picture Seneca standing there in her underwear. I wasn't sure how the fire hadn't eaten away at those garments at the same time as the rest of her

210

clothing. Maybe she had flame retardant undies? I'd heard that she and Brayden had spent only a few hours in the infirmary. Either they'd both refused further treatment or whatever the cube had done to them wasn't that extreme.

"Well, as long as you're keeping them in check, I suppose it's better to have you playing the role of the enamoured girl," Celine said in an airy tone.

I resented the insinuation that I was lovesick. *I am not lovesick. I am an appropriate amount of into Zachary, thank you very much.* Changing gears, I said, "When are you going to tell me what's happening? I think I've proved that you can trust me by now."

"You'll know when the time is right. But I do hope that you've got better control of that shadow magic of yours."

"Considering I managed not to strangle you with shadows for grabbing my arm, I'd say I'm getting a lot better." The bravado in my tone was all I could muster.

"Good. Study up, Norah. You want to be sure you're ready. It could be the biggest test of your whole life."

She started to walk away, but I reached out and snagged her wrist in my fingers. She looked at me with an air of disgust.

"What are you doing? We can't exactly be seen together. That's part of it. People think we hate each other."

"Wonder what gave them that idea," I muttered.

"So, unless you want the whole academy knowing what we are up to, which would ruin everything, let go of my arm or I'm going to electrocute you. Just ask Miranda how long it takes for those kind of burns to heal."

I couldn't stop myself from laughing at her threat. I wasn't saying I was faster than her when it came to magic. I was probably slower than a sloth, but I could still feel the shadows simmering below the surface. They wanted out, and they were hungry to take on my enemy. They got a taste of Celine on Halloween and they wanted more. She might zap me a time or two, but I'd drown her in shadows and smoke before she could do much real damage. And if all else failed, I was more than happy to just slug her in the jaw. Something told me she wasn't much of a physical fighter. Not that any of that mattered—with so many druids on patrol, we weren't going to get very far into any fight before we were found. Not only would I not get the satisfaction of seeing Celine taken down a peg or two, but I'd get myself kicked out of whatever scheme she was cooking up.

"Just answer me one thing, Celine."

"Maybe." She pulled her arm free but didn't walk away.

"Why are you doing all of this? I mean, let's be honest, we both know you've had control over your powers for years. You're basically the queen of this place. So why are you trying to change everything?"

She tilted her chin upward. I couldn't be sure she wasn't trying to look down her nose at me, which kinda made me want to break it.

"That's all true. But that doesn't mean I don't think we deserve better than we've got. Isn't that what a leader does, makes things better for the people they're leading? Just because we aren't druids doesn't mean we are any less worthy of wielding power. They think we're nothing. I bet they would have preferred to not even send their enforcers here. Probably would have preferred we all just fade away. But we aren't going to do that. We won't let them silence us or force us into obscurity anymore."

She flicked her hair over her shoulder and strode off before I had a chance to say anything in response. Her words rang in my ears and I knew she had a point. We were the rejects of society. The unclassifieds. The ones who didn't have a special skill worthy of being nurtured elsewhere. Well, boy were they going to be surprised when four misfits flipped the tables on them.

Chapter Eighteen

April faded into May faster than I could have believed until we were mere weeks away from our first set of final exams—and I still felt woefully under-prepared. I'd made some progress, yes, but was it enough to impress my instructors so they wouldn't fail me? Glover and Rathbone seemed to like me well enough, but that didn't mean they wouldn't be hard arses when it came to giving their exams or handing out grades. The rest of the classes felt like a shot in the dark. I was already convinced I was going to utterly fail Botany.

"You're stress-eating again," Eva noted in a bored tone as I shoved another lemon crème pasty into my mouth.

Technically, we weren't supposed to eat in the library, but what the librarian didn't know wouldn't hurt her. And I was being careful to contain the crumbs. I hadn't intended to be one of those people who shovelled down calories to get through study periods but here we were, and I felt no guilt or shame about it. Better to put on a few kilos instead of losing my mind and consuming the entire campus in shadow or something. That seemed like a fair trade off. Plus, they were delicious.

"Not even sorry," I said around the remnants of my snack, and offered her one. "They're good."

She waved it away and I caught the pallor of her cheeks. Where I went the whole hog on food, she was the exact opposite. If she'd eaten more than a single meal in days, I'd be surprised. What a pair we made. I sighed and set them on the table between us.

"You really should eat something. You're going to faint from low blood sugar, and I feel like one of us should be conscious for long enough to pass these exams."

"I just can't," she groaned and started to gather her books.

"You are going to be brilliant," I promised her. "You are already doing loads better than like half the class."

She stopped mid-motion and shook her head. "I'm not though."

I grabbed her hand and guided her back to her chair. "What is going on with you? This is more than just regular exam nerves."

Unshed tears sparkled in her eyes, making the irises dance with light reflected from above us. "Since Christmas break I can't stop thinking about how my dad is."

"Still no luck in finding him?"

"Mum's written a few times, saying she's getting closer, but I think it just makes things worse. We know I get my magic from him, but not knowing who he is, it's starting to get to me. What if I'm not good enough for him?"

"Stop thinking that way right now," I said sharply. "He would be lucky to call you his daughter, whoever he is. And even if he's the bloody head of the Council or something, you don't owe him anything, Eva."

"You know, you can be quite the motivational speaker when you want to be," she whispered and sniffled.

"Nah, I just hate seeing my best friend feeling like she has to live up to someone who wasn't even around. You might get your magic from him, but he didn't do a damned thing to help shape who you are. Your magic is all you."

"Wise words. Too bad a friend of mine can't seem to listen to her own advice," she said, raising an eyebrow at me.

She wasn't wrong. Even now, as I sat here trying to cram magical knowledge into my brain, I couldn't shake the spectre of Micah's legacy. The sense that I was still in some small way chasing his shadow. I thought I'd made the decision not to be like him over Christmas and yet I could tell Celine's plan was pulling me back in. Why did life have to be so complicated?

Eva was watching me intently, presumably expecting a response to her comment. I sighed.

"I guess good advice is hard to take sometimes. I am trying. I don't know, maybe it would help if I knew what I wanted to do once we were done here."

"You'll figure it out."

"Maybe I should just open that coffee shop," I muttered.

"What?"

I ducked my head and shoved another pasty in my mouth to avoid the discussion. Unfortunately, my roommate was stubborn when she wanted, and she could wait out my sweet tooth. I swallowed and when I looked up, she was still waiting, drumming her fingers on the table.

"It's stupid. Nothing really," I said. Her incredulous expression suggested she thought otherwise. "Okay, fine. Back during the Valentine's Day dance, Zachary and I were just talking, getting to know each other, and he asked me what I wanted to do if I didn't have magic. I told him I'd like to open a coffee shop."

"How'd he feel about it?" she probed.

"He thought it wasn't a bad idea. But it isn't like it matters, what with me scaring him off."

"Maybe he's just sorting out his priorities," she offered.

"Men are stupid," I grumbled, but didn't move. "And I mean, it's not like I need his approval or whatever, anyway."

"Exactly. You don't need anyone's permission to be who you are, and don't you forget it, girl."

She nudged my shoulder playfully and then got up.

"Yeah, I guess," I mumbled.

"Aren't you coming?" she asked when I made no move to get up, and slung her bag over her shoulder.

Unique Magics revision lesson. I'd nearly forgotten that Glover was holding a special session to go over what would be on our final exam and give us a little extra in-class practise before we had to actually sit the exam. Even though she kept saying it was a pass or fail course, I still doubted I'd be receiving a good mark. I'd come a little way, yes, but nowhere near the level of control of my classmates.

I gathered up my books and snacks and trailed after Eva. It wasn't that I disliked Glover's class. But as much as I'd griped about the early mornings on Saturday, I felt safer to explore my own magic with just her around. Call it performance anxiety or whatever, but I hated having to showcase it in front of everyone else. Well, that and my preference for having less targets if my magic went haywire again. Most of the class still gave me a wide berth, anyway. Even Celine and her groupies pretended they hated me. I had to give it to her: when she committed to an act, she really went all in. Or maybe it wasn't an act. I was pretty sure Melinda, at least, wasn't acting. And I knew I wasn't.

Glover stood at the front of the class when we made it in. All the desks had already been pushed aside to the perimeter of the room. Celine, Jessa, and Miranda stood huddled in one corner. Rory watched them, clearly trying to catch Celine's eye. I slunk to the far corner where people usually didn't bother me, and waited for the instructor's instructions.

"Right, let's focus please, everyone. Now, I know you've got more than just my exam coming up. I'm not blind enough to think you're going to devote all of your time to practicing your skills from our classes exclusively. But I want you all to consider how using some of the techniques we've used in this class can benefit your other courses."

It was an interesting thought. I could definitely see how being able to summon and control the shadows within me helped control the electricity we spent so much of Energy Manipulation channelling. I wasn't sure how it helped in much else, though.

"Before we start actually reviewing what we've covered this year, I wanted to share some important information with you that I doubt my colleagues have yet shared. The first shouldn't surprise you. As I noted at the start of semester in September, given the vastly different natures of your magics, this class is pass or fail. The good news is that as long as you've shown some growth in controlling and using your abilities this semester, I'm more than happy to pass you on to your second year."

"So, what's the bad news?" Rory called out.

"Well, as you know, if you fail any of your exams, you will be held back a year," Glover said. "But there have been some changes this year. Should you fail *all* of your exams, or fail to sit them, you will be expelled. And, as you are aware, that will mean your magic will be bound."

Anger crashed over me like a tidal wave. It consumed every part of my mind and drowned out rational thought. It didn't matter if I'd gone to the Council seeking to have my magic bound a year ago. That had been of my own volition. I'd seen how much Micah struggled being locked up without his powers. I couldn't be certain it was the loss of his powers that made him look less than he had been, or if it was just prison life. Probably a mix of the two, but to kick us out and take our magic if we were bad test takers wasn't fair. It was a barbaric punishment.

"They're treating us like criminals," Celine said.

I opened my mouth to agree with her when I caught myself. She'd spent all of this semester still acting like I terrified her. People would notice if I agreed with her sentiments.

"Why didn't the dean or someone tell us that before?"

Rory growled.

"I probably ought to have saved that titbit for the end of our review session," Glover sighed and pinched the bridge of her nose.

"Norah," Eva hissed a warning out of the corner of her mouth.

I looked down to find my hands covered in darkness. Everyone else's gazes fell on me, even though I hadn't spoken. I tried to focus on my breathing to keep it inside, but that just fuelled the anger.

"Tell me, Norah, would letting that anger out make you feel better?" Somehow Glover had materialised next to me.

"Maybe," I answered through gritted teeth.

"Well then, have at it."

I pivoted to stare at her open-mouthed. A few of the other students let out gasps as well. Glover appeared unfazed. She just gestured for me to step into the middle of the room.

"Oh, come now, you all didn't think we would just let a bunch of students just learning to use their powers have at it without any protection?" she chided and gestured to tiny runes high up on the wall.

I spotted them running in an undulating pattern along the walls and down to the floors. How had I been here for so long and not noticed them? My brain decided now was the perfect time to take a trip down memory lane to see if the rest of the lecture rooms bore similar protections.

"Whenever you're ready Norah. Keeping that all bottled up isn't doing anyone any good."

My hands tingled as the shadows twisted and danced along my skin. It wanted to be set free. I just prayed it wouldn't lash out at anyone in particular. I stood there in the centre of the room and stared down at the magic gathering in my palms. I didn't know what I was supposed to do with it other than let it out. It sounded so simple. Just release it…but I'd never done that. Not consciously. And even the times I'd used it as a defence, the shadows had still been part of me, bending to my will. Could I even let them go and detach from me?

I caught Celine staring at me and she mouthed the words 'let go'. Swallowing the fear starting to burn like bile in my throat, I urged the magic to coalesce into a solid mass. Shadow shouldn't have any weight whatsoever and yet it felt like someone had dropped lead into my hands. I stooped to support the weight of it until it was too much to carry, then I drew my hands back and lobbed it at the front of the room.

I expected it to shatter on contact, or maybe leave a giant hole in the wall and keep going into the next lecture room. Instead, the ball collided with a thin, silvery layer of magic about a centimetre and a half away from the actual wall. On contact, the shadow ball flattened, absorbed by the protective magic. My shadows did their best to spread out along the simmering surface, snuffing out whatever light it produced but either the protection runes were insanely powerful or I wasn't that good at this, because the light burned bright like a solar eclipse and swallowed the shadows up inside it.

"Good," Glover said. "Now, how do you feel?"

How *did* I feel?

"Uh, I don't know." I tried to take stock of my physical and emotional state, but I was too overwhelmed by seeing what the runes could do to my magic to make sense of how I felt.

"I have to admit, I haven't seen a first year student channel that much power and still be upright," she said, and patted my shoulder before directing the rest of the class to pair off and practise their skills.

My apparent display of strength earned me the chance to sit down in the corner and ponder my navel. Eva had gone off to partner with some blonde girl whose name I could never remember. Priscilla? Patricia? My temples throbbed at the overuse of my magic, making the exercise of trying to sort out blondie's name pointless. It wasn't important, anyway.

"Glad to see you're learning to harness that power,"

Celine said, and stood in front of me, electricity dancing across her skin.

"Why are you even talking to me?" I sighed.

"They're all distracted. Besides, she told us to practise, and that's what I'm doing," she answered as a perfectly spherical bubble of energy balanced between her palms.

"Congrats," I said dryly.

She rolled her eyes and took a step closer. "I have to admit, I've never seen someone manipulate their unique magic like that before. Giving it weight like that. I hate to say it, but I was impressed."

"Thanks, I guess. I'd never done that before."

She bounced her energy ball from hand to hand and glanced over her shoulder at the rest of the class. No one seemed to pay us any mind. "I just wanted to tell you that you need to be ready. Everything is going to kick off after exams."

"Why then?" I probed.

"Because everyone's guard will be down. All the lecturers will be busy doing grades. And the stupid druids will be too busy trying to control rowdy drunken students. They won't be paying us any mind. Especially not with what you bring to the table."

"Just tell me that this is going to make things better," I said, suddenly exhausted—by my magic, by this plot, by the whole stupid situation.

"It will. No more forcing us into magicless exile if we fail. You have my word on that." She lobbed her energy ball at the wall by my left ear. Too close for comfort. Like my shadows, the protection runes ate up her energy, burning a duller purple as it dispersed her power.

"Change is coming, Norah."

Her words were all I needed to hear. Whatever was going to happen, it would make things better. Micah had gone about things the wrong way. I wasn't going to make the same mistake.

Chapter Nineteen

My penchant for snacking had driven Eva to kick me out of the dorm. She'd eaten a piece of toast and jam before I'd left, so I was satisfied I wouldn't return to a dead roommate. I lay flat on the grass beneath the tree in the courtyard with my eyes closed. I should be studying but my brain couldn't handle any more learning. Besides, it was the practical stuff I struggled with. I was either going to know how to do the magic, or I wasn't.

My ears perked up at the sound of approaching footsteps. With my eyes still closed I couldn't quell the hope that when I opened them, a certain druid enforcer would be standing there with a peace offering for being a total prat and avoiding me like a little bitch. I cracked one eye and that hope died on the vine. Seneca loomed over me.

"You're in my sun," I said, even though the sun was shielded behind the tall branches of the tree above me.

"Don't think I've forgotten about you," she replied, her eyes narrowed.

"You do know how to make a girl feel special."

"You're going to regret attacking me."

"Oh, come on, we both know you were the one being out of order. All I did was ask for help with my bags." I scowled and pushed myself to my feet.

"Touched a nerve, did I?" Her lips twisted into a thin smile.

"Whatever. Look, I was just sitting here minding my own business, not bothering anyone, so I don't know why you felt the need to come over. Don't you have corridors to patrol or decontaminate or whatever it is you do here?"

Another shadow loomed and I turned to see Brayden appear, tugging on Seneca's arm.

"Come on, just leave it. She's not worth it."

His words sounded eerily the same as Zachary's had been when I'd lost control and choked Seneca with my magic. My scowl transformed itself into a frown.

"Hey, where's Zachary been?"

Brayden arched a brow at me. "Keeping track of that airhead isn't my job."

He ushered Seneca back toward the entry to the building. I waited for a count of twenty before I retreated inside. Glancing around, I settled in the alcove where I'd chatted with Kelsey a few weeks ago and I realised, despite not knowing her well, I could use a dose of her support. I pulled the communication stone out of my bag and stared at it. After a solid twenty seconds of cradling it, I was forced to admit I had no idea how it worked.

"Norah, are you okay?" Rathbone's voice drew me away from gazing at the colourful stone.

"Uh, yeah. Fine," I said, trying to hide the stone.

He closed in and my pulse throbbed in my neck. The tiny voice in the back of my head warned me that I wouldn't need to worry about failing my exams if he turned me in for having contraband. Even if I had no clear proof the stone wasn't allowed.

"Is that a communication stone?" his tone was casual, friendly even.

"Um, maybe."

"Haven't seen one of those in ages."

"You know about them?"

"You didn't think they were banned, did you?"

"Well, I don't know honestly."

"It can be hard to be cut off from our families and friends while we're here. I get it."

"Yeah. I've only used it once and the other person contacted me. I'm not sure how to make it work."

He held out his hand, but I didn't hand it over. He must have sensed my hesitation because he gave me a sympathetic look.

"I know I'm just an instructor, but I am trying to help. Exam times are stressful. Having someone to talk to on the outside is a good thing."

I passed him the stone and he summoned a touch of energy, channelling it into the stone. It lit up like it had when Kelsey had contacted me before. "Now, you just need to tell it who you're trying to reach."

"Like their name?"

"Generally that helps."

"What if I don't remember their last name?"

"Having a mental image of them in your mind can help."

I cupped the stone in my hands and watched the colours swirl around, chasing each other. Rathbone cleared his throat and retreated without a word. At least he respected my need for privacy. On the other hand, for all he knew I was about to have a lewd conversation with a lover, and I was pretty sure that was something he wouldn't want to stick around for. I conjured an image of Kelsey from the time we met at the trial and said, "Kelsey".

At first, nothing happened. The colours continued to swirl, but there was nothing to suggest that the connection had been made. Then, all of a sudden, I picked up on a strange humming sound emanating from the centre of the stone. I could hear snatches of voices, but they didn't make sense.

"Hello?" I whispered, being sure to keep the stone in my lap and not shout.

More humming which transitioned into static and then I heard, "Norah? Is that you?"

Kelsey's voice came through as if she was speaking through a barrier. "Yeah, I'm here. Can you hear me?" I asked.

"Hold on."

I waited and the static dissipated. When she spoke again, her voice was as clear as if she was sitting next to me. "I'm sorry about that. Communication can be a bit tricky before you pass through the ward lines."

"Ward lines?" I prompted.

After a long pause, she said, "I was paying Micah a visit."

"Micah? As in my brother? The arsehole who threatened you?"

"Like I said at the trial, I don't blame him for what he did. He was under the influence of someone else. I was just the person he happened to aim his power at."

"Seriously, you are the most forgiving person I've ever met," I offered.

Silence greeted my words. Maybe I shouldn't give her a backhanded compliment like that. I glanced down to see if the stone had stopped vibrating and I'd lost the connection. Did both people need to want to talk for it to work? I should have asked Rathbone for more tips before he'd bowed out.

"I can understand where he's coming from," Kelsey finally offered, her voice quieter now.

"I didn't mean to imply you shouldn't be forgiving of people, it's just, he could have really hurt you," I said.

"Well, I guess we're all lucky he didn't. Really, Norah, he got swept up in everything Raphael was preaching. I don't agree with what he did, but I understand it."

"So, uh, how was he? I haven't seen him since New Year's."

"Subdued. But I think he appreciated my visit. Not that I can tell the Circle that's why I went. They wouldn't have approved."

"Because he's a convicted criminal?" I murmured.

"Because they wouldn't see the point of continuing to associate with someone who has no magic."

"But they throw around revoking people's magic like it's easy and no big deal. I mean, if you fail too many classes here, they kick you out and you get your powers bound."

"I know. And if I'd been allowed to vote, I would have voted against the new changes. They don't help anyone, not really. And I don't disagree with the idea that there needs to be more equality in our society, especially in our justice systems, but revolution is rarely the answer."

"So, what *is* the answer then?"

"I don't know. But I do know it can't come from just one person. For there to be change, people have to see the need for it. They need to be willing to listen to each other and make compromises. That will happen, and when it does, I hope I'm part of it. I could see you being part of it, too."

There was the lightly veiled optimism I was hoping for. I hadn't been anticipating it to come in a discussion about my brother and what he'd been trying to do, but I'd take it.

"That sounds nice," I said with a heavy sigh. "Assuming I don't get kicked out of the academy first."

"You won't," she replied. "You've been working hard and I know you'll get through it."

"I don't know how you can be so sure when I'm barely certain I'll even spell my own name right on the tests."

"Maybe it's because of what Micah did to me, but I feel like... like we're connected. I don't know how to explain it, but I know you can do this. You're not a quitter, Norah. In fact, I think you might be one of the bravest people I know."

"Me? What have I ever done that's brave?" I asked in disbelief.

"You marched into the Circle's headquarters uninvited and made them hear you out to appeal their decision."

"Didn't work though," I reminded her.

"No, but it took a lot of courage to go in there, more courage than most people I know have. More courage than anyone on the council has."

I let her words sink in for a minute. She was right. No one had told me to go and appeal that decision this summer. No one had even told me to make the request in the first place. I'd taken it upon myself to make those decisions and not back down until I had no other choice. And sure, the Circle could be hard arses, using their authority to mete out harsh punishments to people. But the druids weren't all bad. When he was around, Zachary was pretty decent, not to mention a good kisser. And for some reason Kelsey believed in me when she had no reason to. I'd argue she had every reason to hate me given my family ties. But they both believed that I could be something independent of my family and what society thought I'd turn out to be.

Not all druids deserved my ire. Or Celine's, for that matter. And maybe they didn't deserve whatever she had planned. People would get hurt, I was suddenly sure of it—as sure as I was that I couldn't go through with it. I couldn't let people—even druids, and especially one druid—be hurt in Celine's crusade. I had to find a way to stop it.

But I didn't have enough information to stop her outright. I didn't know anything beyond that it was happening after exams. Sure, I could go to the dean and blow the whistle, but there was no proof they'd done anything to break either school rules or the law. And Celine wasn't stupid. She'd deny any wrongdoing, and her cronies would fall in line lest they be punished. No, I'd have to wait and pray that I could stop whatever they were planning when the time came.

"Norah, are you still there?" Kelsey's voice drew me back to the here and now.

"Yeah, sorry. I was just thinking about what you said. You know, I'm glad I met you that day. And as much as I complained about it then, I'm glad they didn't grant my request. I may not be the best witch ever to walk the halls of Braeseth Academy, but I deserve my shot to make my own mark."

"I wish I could be there when you get your exam results, but I don't think my presence would be welcome." I could hear the sad smile in her voice, and wondered why she would be any less welcome than the rest of the druids—and that hadn't stopped them.

Speaking of other druids... "Hey, do you know anything about the druid enforcers who were assigned to do clean-up here? This semester?"

"I know the Circle assigned some people. They were supposed to be dismantling the curses that Raphael's people put on the academy. They've been doing the same at the other academies, as far as I'm aware."

"Do you know if any of them got called back to the

Circle?"

"I'm not sure. Why, is something wrong?"

Eva knew all about my not-quite-relationship with Zachary. But she was my roommate, and it was nearly impossible to keep that sort of thing from her. Could I trust Kelsey with the knowledge, too?

"Nothing wrong exactly. I just sort of became friendly with one of them and now I haven't seen him since February. It's probably nothing, but I'm a little worried about him."

"I don't have anything to do with the law enforcement department, but I could try to look into it if you wanted. I'm not sure what sort of records the Circle will have, but I'm happy to find out what I can." Her voice wavered as she spoke, like she wasn't confident in her ability to pull it off without getting caught. And despite the risk, she was still offering.

"I appreciate the offer, Kelsey, but I don't want to get you into trouble. You've risked a lot for me already and I'm sure I'm worrying for nothing."

"Are you sure? What's his name? Let me look."

I waved my hand even though she couldn't see me. Not having face-to-face conversations with people was annoying.

"You don't have to bother. I promise. I should really be putting my focus on last-minute studying and stuff.

I'm sure I'm just overreacting. It's a bigger campus than you'd expect, and I don't go everywhere all the time. He probably just got reassigned to a different part of the grounds." I was doing a pretty convincing job of talking myself out of my concern about Zachary's absence. After a beat, I added, "Listen, I'm glad you picked up. And that you reached out before. It made me feel not so alone in all of this. You've made me feel almost normal."

"Everyone deserves to have someone they can turn to, no matter what. And everyone has their own stuff they need to work through." Her tone warmed, and I sensed the smile in her voice. "I'm glad I could be that person for you. I should get going. They're expecting me back at headquarters soon. Good luck with your exams, Norah."

The stone stopped vibrating and I exhaled slowly. I stowed it back in the bottom of my bag and stood up, my calf muscles protesting after being crammed in the alcove at such cramped angles for so long. I bent to massage the stiffness out of my body and realised that no one had come through the corridor the entire time I'd been having my conversation. It wasn't totally unusual for there to be less foot traffic at this time of day, but there was usually at least one person coming or going. It was the main path to pretty much everywhere. Which made me curious: had Rathbone somehow warned off anyone who might be coming this way?

I turned my gaze toward the ceiling and then the floor, spotting runic symbols etched into the walls. Had someone's protection spell ensured my privacy? I shook my head. That didn't make sense—there were far more private spaces that could use such a protection. Maybe, if I survived this year's exams, I'd look into runic studies next semester.

I stood there a moment longer, my head swimming with my new perspective. I'd been committed to helping Celine carry out her plan before, but now I knew there was no way I could go through with it. Whatever she was planning, she needed to realise that not all druids were bad. There were people who understood what we were going through and could help make things better—the right way. So, I'd play along until she gave me the full details of the plan. And then I'd stop her.

First, I just had to make it through exams in one piece and with my sanity intact.

Chapter Twenty

By late May, my nerves were a wreck. And the start of exams just made things worse. It wasn't that I felt under-prepared now. I just couldn't shake that it meant I had run out of time to find a way to dissuade Celine from her plans. Granted, I hadn't tried very hard. Or at all. I'd decided it was safer to just interrupt her mid-plan so she couldn't change her mind.

That, of course, meant I needed to be able to actually take her on. As I sat in our magical law final, staring at the short answer questions on my paper, my stomach lurched. The questions weren't difficult. I almost got the sense our instructor gave us easy questions so that most of us would pass, but the content still put me in a bad mood. The fact that failure might mean I lose my place in this world forever loomed like the Sword of Damocles over me. And as I feverishly scribbled down answers, I wondered if things went sideways and I couldn't stop Celine, whether the answers given during this exam would be taken as evidence against me.

"Time is up."

I blinked down at my paper. By some miracle I'd managed to put down some form of response to all of the questions. We wouldn't have our results until over a week from now. So there was little I could do other than hand in my answer sheet with the rest of the class and move on to the next exam.

"That wasn't as bad as I thought it would be," Eva said as she fell into step beside me.

"I guess not. But I still felt like I should have written more," I replied, and shifted my bag to the other shoulder.

"At least we've got Rathbone's exam next. He's already told us we just need to successfully sustain an energy ball for thirty seconds or longer and he'll pass us," she reminded me.

It sounded so easy when she said it that way. But for all I knew, I'd end up creating another shadow weight out of the sheer nervous energy coursing through me. Would he dock points for that? Maybe he'd give me extra credit. It was hard to tell with him.

The tiny hairs on the nape of my neck bristled and I turned to glance over my shoulder. I stopped dead in my tracks when I spotted Zachary watching me from the far end of the hall. So he was still around. Just doing everything to avoid me. Well, fine. Two could play that game.

"What is it?" Eva asked, nudging my arm.

"Just thought I saw someone watching us," I said. She didn't need to know who.

"Keep your mind focused on the task at hand. Boy

troubles can wait until we're free of tests. And partying."

I should have known I couldn't keep what was on my mind from her. Too perceptive by far. I sighed. If only it were that easy. When everyone else was celebrating the end of semester and getting drunk and waiting for their exam results, I had to stop some cryptic plot that I'd foolishly signed up for.

We reached Rathbone's lecture room to find him waiting there with a serious expression on his face. In fact, I couldn't recall him ever looking that stern in the entire time I'd known him. Maybe he disliked final exams as much as the rest of us.

"Leave your bags in the corridor before you come in," he said.

"What's that about?" I whispered as I laid my bag beside Eva's.

"Not a clue, but it doesn't bode well."

The room was set up much like Glover's, with the desks pushed to the far edges. There were little x's on the floor, and he signalled for each of us to stand on one. It seemed a bit over the top to me, but I wasn't going to argue with one of the two instructors who actually liked me.

As soon as I set foot on the mark, my ears popped, and my surroundings vanished. Or at least were so distorted I couldn't see what was going on around me.

But I could still hear. The confused cries of my classmates bombarded my ears as I tried not to let panic set in. Rathbone had set the exam this way for a reason. He wasn't trying to hurt us. I repeated that mantra in my head and took slow, calming breaths until my pulse receded from playing an overbearing drum beat in my temples.

"As I stated in our revision session, your exam for this semester is to produce a sustained energy ball for at least thirty seconds." Rathbone's voice echoed in my little chamber. By the way everyone else went quiet, I suspected they could hear him, too. "You will be given as many tries as needed within the allotted hour. However, do bear in mind that each subsequent try will affect your score. Those who take more than six tries to complete the task will not receive a passing grade."

Great, no pressure, then.

"You may begin."

Not being able to see my classmates proved to be a blessing in disguise. I could concentrate on my own magic in my own time without their judgment. And somehow, the eerie silence around me was soothing. Knowing that I had the full hour to make my attempt, I started by relaxing my body like Glover had taught us. I let the magic pool in my core and spread out through my body until I practically exhaled shadow.

"You can do this," I told myself.

The magic came to me more easily than it ever had before. The electricity danced along my skin, zipping from tip to tip in a rainbow of colours. Staring at it and marvelling at its beauty probably cost me more time than I had to waste, but I'd never produced anything like it before. I shook my head in an attempt to regain my focus, and summoned the magic into my other hand, letting the current build up there until the power crackled along every finger and up my hand to the wrist. It looked almost like my skeleton was electrified with the way it moved and flexed when I waved my hands around.

"Okay, this is pretty cool," I murmured.

Time to form an energy ball. I hadn't succeeded in making a perfect sphere yet. Except the shadow ball I'd formed during Glover's revision lesson. I could do it with this, too. Except I wasn't angry like I had been then. I was more anxious than anything. Drawing on that emotion only proved to make the energy coalesce into glistening goo that stuck to my fingers like honey.

"Thirty minutes remaining," Rathbone's voice echoed in my little chamber.

I shifted to face a different part of the tinted chamber. Not that I expected changing directions would be the fix I needed, but it was enough of a distraction at least to reset my mind. Pulling on the anxiety bubbling below the surface wasn't going to do it. I'd never managed to make magic work when I was feeling anything close to a positive emotion.

I'd tried hard to keep the panic at bay coming into today's exams. I didn't want to get in my own head too much that I'd sabotage myself. But I also couldn't forget that at the end of this particular tunnel waited a Celine-shaped problem. And that still scared me. For good reason. If I didn't stop her, she was going to shatter what little trust existed between us and the druids. If I did stop her, she was going to shatter *me*. I focused on that feeling and the sphere taking amorphous shape between my fingers solidified into a neat sphere with hundreds, maybe thousands, of little connecting branches of lightning. It was just as beautiful as when the energy had just been taking shape on my fingers.

Time to count it out.

"One, two, three, four," I began, going as slowly as I could to ensure I didn't short-change myself.

I expected the sphere to waffle about and weaken the longer I held it there, and yet it sat there perfectly content not to move or waiver in shape. It must have been a fluke that I'd managed it on my first go.

"Twenty-seven, twenty-eight, twenty-nine, thirty, thirty-one, thirty-two, thirty-three…"

By the time I'd made it to a full minute, my neck and

shoulder ached from standing in one position with such intense concentration. I lowered my hands, assuming the energy ball would go crashing to the floor. Instead, it sat there, buoyed by a thin layer of shadows. I hadn't intended to manifest any of my unique magic.

I wasn't sure what came next. I'd completed the task Rathbone had set out for us not long after the half-hour mark. Did that mean I got to leave early? Or was I stuck in this chamber until the hour had passed? And what about the energy ball still hanging suspended mid-air? Was I supposed to reabsorb that power? Or just lob it at one of the walls and wait to see if the same protection spells neutralised it?

I didn't have time to wonder too long before the sides of the chamber vanished. My energy ball plummeted to the floor, sucked up neatly by the x I'd originally stepped on. Rathbone stood in front of me with a clipboard in hand.

"You'll receive your marks next week. Good luck in the rest of your exams."

Going on his statement earlier in the class, it seemed a fair assumption that getting it on the first try meant high marks. I'd actually managed to earn a high mark in something... me. Seriously. I shook my head in amazement, then hurried out of the room and scooped up my bag. As soon as I grabbed it, I noticed the flap was undone, and I was sure I hadn't left it that way. Right? Pushing the paranoia down, I waited for Eva, trying not to spend the time wondering who might or might not have been taking a rummage inside my bag. By the time Eva made it out quarter of an hour later, I'd decided I must have been the one to leave it open. There was no reason anyone would care about my revision notes, that was just ridiculous. And then I took in Eva, and the thought left my mind. She looked worn out and pale.

"Come on, we're going to the canteen and you are eating a proper meal," I said, and dragged her after me.

"We still have one more exam today," she protested.

"In three hours. Plenty of time to get your blood sugar up so you don't pass out doing whatever Weaver throws at us."

I wouldn't put it past the old bat to try to strangle us with plants for our final exam. Then again, I assumed I'd be getting low marks in that class no matter what I did. I just had a black thumb. Maybe shadow magic just wasn't compatible with botany. After all, plants needed light to grow, not darkness. Of course, when I'd voiced that concern to her a few weeks back, she'd told me to stop making excuses, and that my lack of success in her class was down to attitude, not aptitude. But whatever.

The canteen was empty, but the food was still warm. I shoved Eva ahead of me and waited impatiently for her to load up her plate. When I was satisfied she had a respectable first course, we sat down and I swirled around the coffee in my mug. It smelled vaguely of hazelnut.

"So, did you manage it back there?" I leaned forward and watched her every movement.

"Took a few tries but yeah, I managed," she replied.

"How many is a few?" I knew by definition it meant more than two. I'd have wagered it wouldn't have taken her more than once. Maybe twice.

"Four." She hung her head, her hair falling across her face so I couldn't see her embarrassment.

"Hey, that's not so bad. You still passed," I commented. My own excitement at having done it on the first try vanished when I realised that her grade would be significantly lower than mine.

"I think I just froze up. I mean, I've done it hundreds of times, but the whole exam environment and those bloody chambers freaked me out."

"Well, all that matters is you passed. You'll ace the rest of them. You've busted your arse."

"How'd you do?" She looked up, and it was my turn to duck my head in shame. "Come on, Norah. Spill it."

"Don't hate me. I don't honestly know how I did it, but I got it on the first go," I mumbled.

"That's great." I could tell she was trying her best to sound excited for me, but I knew her own struggles must be weighing her down. She met my eye and smiled. "Truly. I'm happy for you."

"So I guess I passed one class."

"Aced is more like it."

"It was a fluke, I'm sure of it. And it didn't happen until halfway through the exam, anyway." I reached across the table and clutched her fingers in mine. "You know you're way better all of this than me, anyway. And it's not a competition between us. I wouldn't have even had half the confidence I had going into that exam if it weren't for you."

"Thanks."

In that moment, I wanted to tell her everything about Celine's plan. I trusted Eva more than I would ever trust Celine. But I couldn't risk throwing Eva off her exam game. I had a couple more days. I could always fill her in once our last exams were done. That way, she would be able to focus on helping me stop things.

"What do you suppose Weaver's going to do?" I said, changing the subject before I could change my mind.

"I heard some second years talking, and they said last year she had them identify a bunch of plants and their uses and properties. Seems pretty simple actually."

"If you can remember that sort of thing."

"At least we know that we've both passed Rathbone's class. And I can't imagine that Glover would fail either of us. You don't see the progress you've made but I do."

"Great. Now I just have to pray for a miracle with the rest of them."

Eva gave me a genuine smile before heading up to get a second plate of food. She returned with one for me, too. As I tucked in, my bag shifted, and something hit my foot. I bent down to find a scrap of paper wrapped around something.

"What is it?" Eva's voice came from above me.

I wrapped my fingers around the paper and object and set them back in my bag. "Nothing important."

I didn't go around leaving notes for myself attached to strange objects. I'd been right: someone had been in my bag during the energy manipulation exam. I doubted it had been Celine or Jessa or Miranda. They'd been in the exam with me. Could it have been Rathbone? But why would he leave me a note? Or maybe it could have been Zachary.

"I need to head back to the dorm for a minute. I'll meet you by the botany lecture room," I said and shouldered my bag.

"Okay. But if you're going to take a nap, you better set an alarm," she called after me.

Sleep was the last thing on my mind. When I got to the dorm, I unbound the paper from the object and studied both. The object was a slender sliver of stone roughly the colour of every stone surface in this place. Determining where it had come from would take forever. I wouldn't know where to even begin looking. I turned it over in my hands and could see some sort of etching on it. A partial rune, maybe? I hadn't a clue. I set it aside and looked at the message, which was a little less subtle.

Watch your back.

Chapter Twenty-One

Most of the rest of my exams were a bit of a blur, except for Botany. I was pretty sure I'd bombed that one in spectacular fashion. I'd been trying to encourage a little plant to grow and it kept wilting every time I touched it. That stupid plant had haunted my dreams for a couple of nights, chasing me through the halls of the academy with its sad-looking, shrivelled leaves and root system trying to strangle me. Maybe it was a harbinger of what was coming.

The day after the third years finished their final exam, Celine cornered me in the library. Her eyes glittered with excitement, which only made my stomach sour more. I wasn't looking forward to going up against her and her cronies to stop their plan, but I had no other choice. I wasn't going to stand by and let them hurt people or set shit on fire.

"You're perky," I muttered as she plunked down in the seat beside me.

"It's time. Tonight, everything changes." Her voice came out in a whisper, but it barely contained her glee.

I sat straighter and leaned in closer to her, hoping my body language signalled interest in her plan, rather than my determination to stop her.

"Does that mean you're actually going to fill me in

what we're doing?"

"You really need to learn some patience," she said.

"I have been patient. Since Valentine's Day, I've been waiting, not asking questions. I've kept my mouth shut. If it's really happening tonight, don't you think I ought to have some idea what I'm supposed to do?"

To make sure I could actually do whatever she needed me to do. It couldn't have escaped her notice that I wasn't exactly the best witch on campus. I didn't need her deciding I wasn't worth being included after all and ditching me because I was awful at magic.

"Would you relax? You're going to know what you need to know when you need to know it." She patted my knee in an overly patronising gesture that made me want to remove her hand at the wrist. "And don't worry, I'm confident you can do what we need you to do."

"I'm not exactly good under pressure. Things tend to go off the rails. Or have you forgotten when my magic manifested on Halloween?"

"God, you're being super needy right now, Norah," she groaned. "All you need to know is we're meeting at ten o'clock tonight in the entry hall. Don't be late, and make sure you aren't followed."

She refused to tell me anything else before she flounced away, leaving me to mentally prepare for every eventuality. I wasn't good at handling that much stress. I ended up in the kitchen cradling a bowl of ice cream an hour before dinner.

"Am I late?" Eva joked and joined me. She dipped a spoon into the melted chocolate mess in the bowl without asking. I didn't argue.

"Right on time," I answered, and shoved the rest of the soupy mixture to her.

At least she'd been eating more since exams ended. The present situation excluded, my binge-eating had returned to normal levels, too. But you couldn't blame a girl for maintaining healthy sugar levels right before trying to thwart evil plans. We sat there shoulder to shoulder in silence for a few minutes before she set the bowl aside and pushed her plait over one shoulder.

"You've got something on your mind. As your best friend, it is my duty to be your sounding board. So, spill."

If only I could.

"I've just got a lot on my mind. Exams might be done, but that doesn't mean our futures are set. I mean, do they really have to keep us waiting in agony like this? Can't they just assign grades immediately and put us out of our misery?"

Her dark brows furrowed and her eyes tightened. I caught the nostril flares and instinctively tried to catch a whiff of myself. I wasn't lying, that stuff was bothering me, but it wasn't what was really preoccupying my mind.

Could she tell that much now? It stood to reason that as we learned to control our powers, they would expand and grow. I was pretty sure my brother hadn't come out of the womb—or puberty—being able to suck the energy right out of people. It had developed over time.

"I agree that the waiting sucks," Eva said carefully, watching me through cautious eyes, "but this is more than just anxiety over grades. Whatever's eating at you is like a bright neon sign. And even you wouldn't mope forever about a guy, so don't tell me it's about Zachary."

She wasn't leaving me much choice except to come clean. But telling her now would risk her going to Bevan before I could stop Celine and company in the act. It wasn't that I wanted to be the one to bust them, but I didn't want them trying to retaliate against my best friend. If there was retribution to be had, it was better if it was directed only at me.

"You're right," I said slowly, not meeting her gaze. "Something is going on, but I can't tell you what it is. I'm sorry."

"Norah, I'm your best friend. You can trust me."

"You are. And I do. But you have to trust me here. Something's not right on campus and I'm so close to figuring out what it is. Like, as close as it's all going to be dealt with by tomorrow."

"You don't have face whatever it is alone."

She wasn't making it any easier to keep her out of this. And she wasn't wrong about me facing off against three girls who were far more in control of their magic than I was—or could hope to be.

"Look, if I'm not back to the dorm by half eleven, you have my permission to come looking for me."

"Not a second longer," Eva said, fixing me with a determined stare.

Now I just had to hope I could derail Celine's plan before my time ran out.

* * *

Waiting until ten o'clock was agony. Checking the time every five minutes nearly drove me mad and I couldn't stop spinning more and more outlandish scenarios through my head as the time ticked past. Finally, at ten minutes to, I crept into the corridor, hoping I'd see Celine or Miranda or Jessa, but only silence greeted me. And darkness.

The quiet grated on my nerves, making me jump every time my heels hit the stone floor. But the dark wasn't scary. It felt welcoming, like it offered some level of protection. My fingers twitched as the deeper shadows in the alcoves called to me. I could almost see them undulating, reaching out to me. Like it was calling to my magic. *Is this what it's like for the druids?*

By the time I reached the entry hall, I was on high

alert. I knew that the druid enforcers were supposed to patrol the halls at night. At least, that had been their routine the rest of the semester. Yet I hadn't met a soul on my way down. If I wasn't already on high alert, their conspicuous absence would have sent my senses into overdrive.

"I was starting to think you weren't going to show," Celine crooned from the small vestibule near the doors to the lecture hall.

"You told me to show up at ten. It's ten and I'm here," I hissed back. "Now, are you going to tell me what the hell we're doing?"

Bright blue tendrils of electricity danced along her hands like ethereal henna paint, marking her skin with elaborate patterns. Under other circumstances, and with different people, I would have thought it was beautiful. I shook myself out of the reverie and waited for her response. Jessa and Miranda huddled closer to Bevan's office door.

"I told you, we're going to change things around here," Celine answered. Jessa retreated to our position.

"He's definitely in there."

"You're going to what, attack the dean?" I asked.

"Not exactly. We're just going to do a little spell that's going to make sure the druids can't ruin our lives anymore."

"Can't wait to see their faces," Jessa giggled.

"You can't believe Bevan's going to let you march in there and do whatever you want," I objected.

"Obviously not. That's where you come in. It's late, and it's very cloudy out tonight. So cloudy it might even block out all the lights. We just need you to give us cover."

"I'm not a fog machine," I grumbled.

"Tonight you are," she said, her eyes hardening. "You give us the protection of not being seen and we make the world stand up and listen. We aren't going to be the world's afterthought anymore."

"And what makes you think Bevan won't know it was me? Last time I checked, I'm the only one with shadow magic on campus," I said, placing myself between them and the door to the dean's office.

"You won't even be in the room. All you need to do is create a barrier, so he can't see us, and we'll handle the rest."

"And what exactly are you going to be doing?" I was stalling, and the way her gaze narrowed as the electricity danced over her skin told me she knew it.

"I told you she would wuss out," Jessa said.

"My magic is unpredictable. I can barely control it on a good day, and I don't need you three being pissed at me because it went haywire and messed with whatever you're planning," I said, hoping she'd believe me.

"Norah's right," Celine said, and nodded toward the door to Bevan's office. "There's a little bauble in his office that controls the protection spells on campus. I'm certain it's linked to his magic, so we'll need his cooperation. Or at least his hands to activate it. Then we're casting our own protection spell. Anyone with druid blood will no longer be welcome on campus. And since they won't know who it was, they'll blame the dean, and they'll have no choice but to send someone new in to replace him. Someone who understands what we're really capable of."

The little blue sphere behind his desk. I'd barely noted it the handful of times I'd been in his office. I'd always been more focused on not getting expelled. I hadn't considered that it was anything more than decorative. I hated to admit it, but Celine's plan was smart. It was still going to fail, but it was smart.

"I'll try my best," I promised, and shook my arms out at my sides.

Dark tendrils laced themselves around my hands, rippling out to form a latticework around me. It had never come this easily before. Not even when it had erupted from me and nearly choked out Celine and her friends on Halloween. Piece by piece, it extended from the floor to the vaulted ceiling. I turned and extended my arms out toward Jessa. She gave a soft yelp before disappearing.

"Nice work," Celina said and marched forward, keeping my wall of shadow between her and the door. The weave of the magic was loose enough for her to see where she was going without walking into anything.

Come on, Norah, get it together.

Psyching myself up to stop her wasn't working as well as I'd hoped. The fact my magic responded to what she needed was worrisome. What if the magic within me had a mind of its own and it wanted the druids gone, even if I'd come to realise that not all of them were bad?

The door to Bevan's office creaked open and I could see him bent over some papers on his desk. He didn't even look up. Either he was used to doors opening of their own accord, or he couldn't see us coming.

"Get it." Celine's voice was barely audible behind my shadow shield.

I watched as Jessa reappeared enough for me to track her movements. She plucked the sphere from behind Bevan's desk and passed it to Celine. Time to make my move. I pictured the latticework unwinding and wrapping around them, constricting their movements. Slowly, patches of shadow unwound themselves, leaping out toward the other girls.

"What are you..." Celine hissed before shadows

clamped her mouth shut.

The room's dim light seemed far too brilliant as my shadows turned their attention to stopping Celine and the others. It was enough to show me that Bevan wasn't bent over out of concentration. He was slumped over. Shit. I stepped up beside him and pressed the tips of my fingers to his throat. He was breathing, but it was shallow.

Before I could convey his condition to the others, something blazed like a ray of sunlight above my head. Something etched in the stones. My shadows retreated so quickly it knocked the air from my lungs. Celine's electricity, which I hadn't even noticed trying to fend off my power, was sizzling, and I watched as it scurried back to her fingertips, leaving little burn marks as they disappeared.

"What the hell was that?" she growled, rounding on me.

"You may be the queen bee around here, but you aren't that smart," I replied. "Did you really think I'd go along with your plan to take over the academy? You're prejudiced just like they are. You just think you're entitled to it because you're the bottom of the food chain."

"She's not the only one who needs to improve their attention to detail, filthy misfit," Seneca's voice retorted from the doorway.

I pivoted slowly, trying to call my shadows back to

me, but it was like I'd never had them in the first place.

She clucked her tongue at me and pointed upwards. "You won't be doing any more magic in here. You don't have the power. But we do."

She cupped her hands together to form a swirling fireball and then launched it straight at my face.

I dived to the floor, dragging Celine down with me. We hit the ground with the heavy thud. It wasn't that I'd suddenly decided to like her, but the nasty hole left in the curtains on the far wall suggested that Celine would have been a corpse if I hadn't saved her.

"I thought you didn't hate druids now," Celine huffed as she tried to shove me aside.

"There are still some arseholes who need to be dealt with. How about we call a truce and kick her arse?" I offered.

"This doesn't mean I like you," she said, and I could smell the ozone around her as she fought to call her magic to the surface.

"Doesn't mean I like you either," I responded, and belly crawled toward the nearest drawer in Bevan's desk. I yanked the bottom drawer open and groped around until I found something long and metal: a letter opener.

I tossed the letter opener over the desk before ducking back down out of range. It clattered harmlessly to the floor, but a quick glance confirmed it had done what I needed it to. It had forced Seneca back enough to give us a chance to get out of the office and into the hall, where our powers might actually work. I'd anticipated a fight tonight, but not like this.

Not a fight for my life.

Chapter Twenty-Two

I didn't check to see if Celine and the others were behind me. I scrambled to my feet and scooped up the letter opener. Seneca expected us to fight with magic, knowing full well we weren't trained. Not like her. Well, there were other ways to fight.

The moment I stepped out of Bevan's office, a weight lifted, and my magic came roaring back as if someone had forced me into a straitjacket and I'd just wriggled free. I latched on to the darkness swirling around me and threw up a barrier to conceal myself.

"Hiding in the shadows isn't going to save you," Seneca taunted from up ahead.

I didn't reply, just took off at a clip, following her voice while it bounced against the stone walls. I didn't pay attention where she was leading us until a zap of electrical current crashed into my back. My shoulder muscles seized, and the sudden jolt of pain made me stop. I spun to find Celine standing behind me, looking out of breath and pallid.

"Don't tell me you're the one wussing out now," I said.

She gestured to our current surroundings. "Look where we are. The cursed corridor. We can't go in there."

Her words gave me pause. I took a moment to look

around and realised that we were in fact in the same corridor I'd followed Zachary to on Valentine's Day. Where I'd saved Seneca and Brayden, who were now repaying that act with one of violence. Zachary had been so sure he'd cleared the curse from this area, but I'd seen their magic turn on them. Unless…could that all have been an act?

"How much do you know about the curses used on the academy?" I whispered.

"I don't know," she answered. "That they were really terrible."

"They were designed to drain people's magic and turn it on them," Eva's voice said from the stairwell.

I whirled to face my roommate. "What are you doing here?"

"I know you said half eleven, but I got a bad feeling and I followed you. You can be mad at me later."

"Isn't the curse cube supposed to leave people really messed up after, too?" I said, gladder than I could say that my friend had ignored me—and terrified for her, too.

"Yeah. So I've heard."

"Well, Seneca and Brayden were out of the infirmary real fast after Valentine's Day. What if they'd faked it to try to convince everyone else there was a bigger threat still on campus than there really was?"

"I was there, though. That looked real."

"They're enforcers, they've studied magic a lot longer than we have. I'm sure they could work a spell to make it look like their magic was causing damage to them."

"Even so, you think Zachary was fooled by them?"

I didn't have time to answer before I went staggering into Celine and Miranda, knocking them down. The shadow barrier I'd been fuelling sputtered and died. The scent of singed material filled my nostrils, and pain seared over my flesh. I rolled over onto my back, gasping. I'd been hit with a fireball.

Footsteps echoed against the stone floor. Seneca appeared, balancing fireballs in each hand. Brayden stood beside her, swirling vortexes of water cupped in his palms.

"We were going to wait until the runes finished you pathetic misfits off, but having a few less to suck dry will make it go faster," Seneca sneered.

"You can't possibly believe we're going to let you get away with this," Eva said, stepping up to put herself between them and the rest of us.

"What naïve words. You can barely sustain an energy ball between the lot of you," Brayden said, his voice low.

I pushed myself to my feet and squared my shoulders. "See, you're the reason we can't trust more druids. You see us as expendable because we aren't exactly like you. Well, guess what, you prick, you're wrong. We deserve this power just as much as you."

Shadows wound their way up my arms and around my torso, hardening with every word I spoke, preparing for the next blow to come. "We put our trust in you, whether we wanted to or not. You were here to undo the damage, and you just made it worse. You aren't above the law either."

"You think we're anything like that maniac?" Seneca snarled, launching another fireball at me.

Electricity filled the air as Celine raised both hands, catching the fire in a net made of branching lightning. The fire leapt at her through her impromptu cage but didn't touch her flesh. I watched her fight it, her hands trembling more and more as she failed to contain the heat. All at once, a low hum filled my ears and her electrical cage snapped out of existence. The fire crawled up her arms and she screamed.

Miranda covered her mouth with her hand and shuffled back, clearly not up to the fight. But Jessa reached out a hand, her fingers outstretched, and one of Brayden's watery vortexes shot from his hand and landed on Celine's burned flesh. The burns sizzled and Celine collapsed to the floor, Jessa darting forward to catch her friend. That left me and Eva to face them ourselves. And

I was the only one with an active power. *Fantastic.*

I had to believe that Seneca had activated one of the power dampening runes hidden around the corridor. If they'd spend as much time here as I thought, they'd likely inscribed them everywhere to give themselves the advantage. Brayden still looked stunned Jessa had been able to steal his water from him without being near him. I used that distraction to my advantage and slipped the letter opener to Eva.

"What am I supposed to do with this?" she whispered, her lips barely moving.

"Find any rune you can and scratch it out. I'll do my best to cover you."

I didn't know much about runes, but I knew enough to be certain that if the rune wasn't perfect, it wouldn't work. I turned my back on her. Time to see what this shadow magic could really do. I held my hands out in front of me and pictured a perfectly spherical mass of inky darkness forming from nothing. I opened my eyes to find it ready and waiting. A flick of my wrist sent the ball hurtling right at Seneca's stomach.

"That's for trying to kill us."

In my periphery, I watched Eva press herself against the wall, letter opener in hand. She needed more than just me distracting them. She needed the cover of shadows. I'd never draped anyone in magic before, but somehow that seemed the logical step. With one hand clenched behind my back, I drew on the power singing in my veins to be released and tried to give it form and purpose: protect Eva.

Before my eyes, my friend's face vanished. The only hint of her presence was the small scratch marks that appeared at random on the walls. I was so focused on making sure Eva was protected, I made a juvenile mistake, and left myself wide open for their attacks.

Water smashed into me, sending me flying down the corridor, followed by a wall of flame. I sputtered, clearing the water from my mouth, and scrambled to my feet again. I stayed low this time, hoping it gave them less of a target as I studied the way they moved around each other, almost orbiting each other.

"They're going to laud us for taking you out," Seneca crooned as Brayden sent another jet of water my way.

Her fire followed a second later, but I was ready this time. I threw up a shadow barrier, letting the ethereal magic swallow theirs. Around the edges of my spell, I saw Seneca glancing upward, sparking something with a snap and a tiny bit of flame drifting upward. Her magic fuelled the runes to dampen and feed off our magic. But if she couldn't see where they were, then she couldn't trigger them.

A plan formed in my head as I watched the druids

advancing on me. They wanted me to give in and give up. They wanted to batter me with magic they didn't think I could handle. And there was a time I would have believed they were better faster, stronger, *better* than me. But I wasn't helpless. I wasn't the best at any of this, but I'd paid attention and I'd learned. And maybe those early morning sessions with Glover had paid off more than I thought.

My heart thumped double time against my breastbone and my mouth went dry as they closed in. I was scared and given the situation, it was probably the first sensible reaction I'd had all day. I held tight to that feeling and channelled it outward. Thick plumes of smoky power filled the corridor, bumping against the walls and crawling up like they had a mind of their own. Seneca might have fire, but I had smoke, and I was going to choke their spells out of existence.

"Stop her!" Seneca spat at Brayden.

I raised a hand and tiny cords of darkness shot from my palms, wrapping themselves around his wrists, binding them together. He struggled against my magic and for once, I was stronger. He tugged and twisted and yet they didn't yield. I'd never had this level of control over my magic before, and it felt *good*. The amped up power coursing through me left me giddy, like I could do anything. I caught movement to his left and watched as

Eva's hand appeared amidst the darkness to slap a cuff on his wrist.

I didn't want to know where she'd got the suppressor cuffs, but I wasn't going to look a gift horse in the mouth. The metal bracelets sealed snugly around his wrists, and I lifted him off his feet, slamming him into the nearest wall until he landed on the floor with a moan. He didn't move again.

"You picked on the wrong misfit," I said, letting the shadows buoy me toward Seneca. I couldn't tell where the ceiling began or where the walls ended, but I knew I was surrounded by my own magic and it was begging for a directive. It needed to be used. It would be so easy to let it smother Seneca until she stopped breathing, but I wouldn't give them the satisfaction of being like the people who'd sparked this bloody war. She had to be stopped, but there was more than one way to subdue someone.

"Cuff her," I said and watched as Eva moved through the haze to slam the other cuff on Seneca's wrist. The flames in her hand were snuffed out immediately and she dug her nails into her skin, trying to pry the cuff free.

"You can't stop us. We're going to eradicate your kind," Seneca snarled. Her nails drew blood, but the cuff remained in place. Interesting that two cuffs worked independently of each other. I filed that away for later investigation.

"You're an army of two and you just got your arses handed to you by a bunch of first years. Trust me, people are going to remember you, but only for being the failures you are."

Shadows lapped at her legs, twisting around her body like a snake going in for the kill.

Out of nowhere, Eva slammed a fist into Seneca's jaw, sending her staggering sideways. She collided with a shadow-draped wall and slid down it. Like Brayden, she let out a groan but didn't get up again.

I smirked at my roommate. "Remind me not to get on your wrong side. That's one hell of a right hook."

Around us, the shadows vanished with a whoosh of air. I gasped, as if someone had knocked the air from my lungs. I'd never had my magic leave my body like that before, and it *hurt*. I half expected Zachary to appear from the dimness to catch me and tell me what a good job I'd done. But of course he didn't. He'd been missing in action for weeks now. He'd made it clear he wanted nothing to do with me. Fantasising about him coming to my rescue was just that, a childish fantasy.

"You were pretty badass yourself," Eva said—and then my knees gave out and I crumpled to the floor, shattering any badass illusions I might have given her.

"I'm going to get help. Just stay here," she promised

and disappeared as the unpleasant greyness of forced unconsciousness began to tunnel my vision.

"Not planning to go anywhere," I offered feebly as her footfalls receded down the stairs.

I had enough consciousness left to spot Jessa still cradling Celine's motionless form. Even in the natural shadows cast by the windows, I could see the angry red burns on Celine's forearms. Jessa had got water on the wounds within seconds, but I knew magical wounds were harder to heal than mundane ones. Miranda must have split at soon as the spells started flying. Coward. She'd been nothing more than a leech to Celine's popularity, pretending she mattered because Celine blessed her with a moment's attention. That wasn't what a true friend did. At least Jessa had tried to help.

I wondered if Dean Bevan had recovered, if taking out Brayden and Seneca had stopped all of their runes from sucking away the magic from the academy. The reality of what they'd tried to do settled like a chill over my body. They'd been trying to take our magic as a way to ensure there could be no insurrection. They'd been willing to strip us of the very thing that made us witches, all because we weren't the same as them. That nugget of rebellion deep within me flared for a brief moment before the exhaustion set in. There would be plenty of time for outrage when I wasn't about the pass out.

This was not at all how I'd imagined the year would end. I doubt even Kelsey, with all her infinite optimism for others, could have predicted I would have taken on two powerful druids and won. How had I gone from the girl who didn't want her powers, to stopping two plots with the potential to lead to a full-blown war? I wasn't supposed to be *that* girl. I was supposed to be the girl no one noticed because I wasn't special.

It was kinda ironic that my shadow magic, which should have kept me hidden, had cast me into the spotlight.

Chapter Twenty-Three

I never thought magic burn-out was a real thing until I woke in the infirmary with the worst headache and body chills I'd ever experienced. Despite the late spring temperatures, I huddled beneath the blankets, burrowing as far down as I could to conserve body heat.

"Norah, are you awake?" Eva's voice came through the curtain to my right.

Part of me wanted to ignore her and go back to sleep for the foreseeable future, but I was grateful she'd helped, no questions asked.

"Yeah," I mumbled from beneath my blankets. "I feel like death, though."

The curtain swished and I rolled over to find my roommate standing there with a bandage on her arm but looking no worse for wear. *Lucky her.* She pulled up a chair and settled beside my bed.

"Guess that's what happens when you throw around as much magic as you did. If it's any consolation, Celine looks like hell, too."

It made it only slightly less shitty, but I forced a smile at my roommate. "Thanks." I adjusted the blankets around me and asked, "Have they said anything about what's going to happen to us?"

"Not yet." She scooted the chair closer, the feet

scraping against the floor. "I still can't believe you were going to go along with her plan that whole time and you never said anything."

"Guess I'm better at keeping secrets than I thought. Not going to lie, it was hard keeping that from someone who can literally sniff out a liar."

"I'm glad you changed your mind about going through with whatever they were planning."

"Me, too."

At least I hoped that would be the way the dean and whoever showed up from the Circle saw it. Eva reached over, snaked her hand beneath the blankets, and gave my hand a squeeze. At least she wasn't abandoning me—which was more than I deserved after keeping her in the dark all year.

We sat there for a while—I think she was trying to lend me some body heat without it getting super weird—but I was happy to have her there. And the longer she sat, the more the chills and the aches receded. At some point, her hand disappeared from mine and I was alone in the silence. Closing my eyes, I tried to pick up on what was happening around me. The low murmurs of the nursing staff came through the curtains, and I caught Celine's name a couple of times.

I was so intently focused on trying to hear their conversation that I missed the impending footsteps until their owner appeared on my side of the curtain. A woman in Council garb I didn't recognise. "Norah Sheehan?"

I sat up a little straighter, smoothing my hair—as if looking presentable was going to help me now. I swallowed. "Yes."

"Please come with me."

I slid from beneath the covers, and she retreated beyond the curtain to let me get dressed in the academy uniform someone had left for me. I suppose if I was about to be expelled, I ought to get one last use out of the clothes. As I left the infirmary, my gaze slid over Celine still lying in bed, her arms bandaged up to the elbows. I'd gotten off easy in all of this so far. Things could have been a lot worse. For us all.

The woman was silent as a stone as she led me through the corridors down to Dean Bevan's office. I didn't try to make conversation, unable to think of anything beyond what might be coming. And whatever it was, I knew I deserved it. She held the door open for me and when I stepped through, I found Dean Bevan sitting behind his desk like every time I'd been there, but this time he wasn't alone. Councilman Hutton hovered at his left shoulder. He had the same haughty expression he'd worn during Micah's trial. I sat, even though no one told me I had to.

"Ms Sheehan, I want you to please tell Councilman

Hutton what transpired last night." Dean Bevan's voice was calm and far more collected than I would have been in his position. More collected than I was right now. I wondered if I could get away with lying.

"Uh, well, me and some other students realised there was something odd going on around the deans' office. We decided to investigate, and we found Brayden and Seneca had been setting runes around the academy. They said they were for our protection, but they weren't—they were taking our power and had been for a while. We had to stop them."

"Anything else?" The dean's narrowed gaze and the turned down corners of his mouth were all the information I needed. I was going to have to rat out Celine and her friends for what they'd been about to do. I'd planned to do it…but I hadn't expected it to be so hard. After everything we'd been through, it felt like a betrayal, and not the sort she deserved.

"Well, I sort of, um, found out about this other plan to take over the academy. They just wanted to be treated fairly, but I stopped them from doing anything dangerous."

Sure, I owed most of that interruption to Seneca and Brayden's runes messing with our powers, but it was still technically true. Hutton stared down his nose at me and for a split second that distrust of druids flashed across my mind and my vision went grey at the periphery.

"Your efforts to thwart what was done here are commended," Dean Bevan said.

"I don't know if I deserve that," I mumbled before I thought better of it.

"Why not?" Hutton leaned forward, ready to hang me with my own admission.

"Because until a few weeks ago, I didn't think Celine's idea of finding a way to get those of us who are relegated to this academy treated with more dignity was such a bad idea."

"But you determined at some point those ideals weren't worth fighting for?" Hutton's brows arched to the point they almost disappeared into his hairline.

"I still think the ideals are worth it, but I could tell Celine and her friends wanted to make changes that could hurt people in the process. And I couldn't let that happen. The other stuff with the druids was sort of luck."

"Well, it seems the girl who never wanted her powers has become quite the hero," Hutton said, curling his upper lip.

"I never asked for any of this," I spat back.

Dean Bevan let out an exaggerated cough to quell any further argument, and I pressed myself to the back of the chair, preparing myself for punishment. They might be commending my part now, but they couldn't just overlook what I'd originally been willing to do, could they?

"Look, if you're going to expel me or lock me up or whatever, just say so," I snapped.

"We have no plans to expel you, Ms Sheehan," Dean Bevan answered.

"You don't?" I frowned. "But I broke a bunch of academy rules."

"Don't be ungrateful," Hutton growled.

God, what a prick.

"Council Hutton here assures me that the two druids you thwarted were not acting on the Circle's order. In fact, they were operating without the knowledge and consent of their own instructors. It would appear that they, too, had become radicalised," Dean Bevan said.

"So, what happens now?" I locked eyes with Hutton, willing him to blink first. A small kernel of satisfaction grew deep within me when he backed off.

"We will be sending hex breakers over the summer to ensure all traces of all the curses have been removed from the grounds. And we will be vetting them thoroughly to ensure they are loyal."

I didn't like the word loyal. Or at least not what he implied when he used it. His mouth hung open slightly, as if he hadn't finished speaking but had forgotten his next words.

"Once the campus has been cleared, the druids will be receding from Braeseth's affairs. The faculty and student body will be able to govern themselves. We do not want any further unrest."

Now I was the one with my mouth agape. I hadn't expected them to just pull out entirely. The small measure of relaxation on Bevan's face revealed he was grateful for the fact he wouldn't have to house other people's soldiers.

"What will happen to Celine and the others?" I couldn't believe I actually cared about the girl who'd made my time here as uncomfortable as possible, but I couldn't help the niggle of concern inside me.

"The druids will be jailed for their part in the attack on the academy. Your fellow students will face trial before the Circle. As for their continued attendance at Braeseth, that remains in the hands of Dean Bevan. If, of course, their powers are not bound as punishment."

Given how they treated my brother's trial, I didn't trust them to grant leniency or take into account that at least Celine had helped stop the druid attack. "That isn't fair. They didn't actually do anything."

"You do not have to like our legal system, Ms Sheehan," Hutton said, "but it exists for a reason. And those who seek to break the laws as they stand now must suffer the consequences."

279

"Well, if you're going to try them, then you'd better count me in, too. I'm just as culpable as them."

"You worked to stop their agenda. You may feel a sense of guilt, but you did not in fact break any laws. They attempted to stage an assault on this institution," Bevan argued. His unspoken plea to quit while I was ahead was as obvious as a flashing sign.

"Listen to your dean, Ms Sheehan," Hutton replied. "Given what your family has gone through, I would think you'd prefer to accept the praise being offered."

"You can't just throw them to the wolves. They helped to stop a larger plot, one you claim was enacted under your nose. It would be pretty bad PR if that got out. The almighty Circle missed the warning signs that their own people were robbing innocent kids of their powers before they could even learn to use them properly to defend themselves. It would make Raphael's cause look a little less crazy." I clamped my jaw shut before I could say anymore. From the look on Hutton's face, bringing up Raphael might have been a mistake. But a bigger one would have been not standing up for someone who'd just wanted the freedom to live life on her own terms.

Hutton's chest puffed out and then deflated as he considered his response. I could picture the tiny gears in his mind whirring as he chose his words. "Fine. You have my word that I will do what I can to ensure leniency. No more than six weeks in a minimum security facility, and no permanent binding."

"And they will be permitted to return to the academy come fall semester, assuming they all pass their exams," Bevan added.

I was a little surprised Bevan was willing to let them come back to the academy, given what they'd tried to do, but maybe he was banking on them rethinking things if they knew he'd fought for them to stay. It seemed a little naïve to me, but what did I know? I was just the outcast unclassified sister of a convicted traitor.

I turned to Hutton. "I'll be there every day of those trials and if they get even a day more, you're going to find yourself with that pesky PR problem."

"Mind your tongue," he snarled.

I pushed myself out of the chair. "Believe me, I don't want to go there. I just wanted to get through this year and learn to use the magic you wouldn't bind. Yes, I'm glad now you refused that request, but that doesn't mean I want to be the centre of attention. The spotlight isn't for me. So, as long as you keep your word and give Celine and her friends a second chance, I can comfortably stay in the shadows and no one has to know."

"You can go," Bevan said, presumably before I could ruffle Hutton enough that he decided to forego all the trials and just lock me up in Daoradh on principle. Probably for the best. I'd never been great at knowing when to keep my mouth shut. But I'd meant what I said. If he went back on his word, all bets were off.

The woman who'd escorted me stepped aside to open the door. I left the office and instead of heading back to the dorm, I headed to the courtyard to sit beneath the tree that me and Eva had claimed as our own. I stretched out on the grass and let the shoots caress the back of my knees and legs. Assuming I hadn't totally botched my exams, this place would be my home again next year. It hadn't gone at all how I'd expected it to, and there were still so many unanswered questions. What would Mum and Dad have to say about what I'd done? It hadn't been the same as Micah, but I'd taken a stand for something I believed in and fought for it. What would he have to say about it, for that matter? Would the Circle even let me in to see him again?

"Am I interrupting?" Kelsey's voice ripped me from my musings.

I sat up to find her standing there in the flesh. "Uh, no. I didn't know you were here."

She sat beside me. "Councilman Hutton insisted I come along. I'm not sure why, since he's spent all year trying to get me removed from my position, but I'm sure he has his reasons."

I frowned. "I hadn't realised things were so tough for you at the Circle."

I hadn't actually thought anything, beyond the fact that she seemed to be the only druid who wasn't a total arse. I'd never considered her life might not be quite as glossy as it seemed.

"Oh, it's nothing, really. Just old prejudices. I knew things weren't going to be easy for me there, but that's not enough to stop me doing what's right." She gave me a wry smile. "I hadn't imagined it would involve spending so much time making tea."

"Well, you'll probably going to be the one Hutton directs all of his pent up rage at. Sorry about that, in advance. I sort of, uh, blackmailed him a little."

Her cheeks flushed and she covered her mouth with both hands. "You didn't."

I held my thumb and first finger an inch apart. "Just a touch."

"I'm so sorry all of this happened."

"Not your fault," I answered with a shrug.

"That doesn't mean I can't be sorry about it. I'm glad you were able to stop it though. I knew things happened for a reason."

I cocked my head and fixed her with a healthy dose of side-eye. "Are you really trying to tell me that they denied my request *twice* just so I would be here to stop some batshit crazies from stealing magic and starting a war?"

"Not in so many words, no, but I did keep telling you that you were worth believing in. You took something that could have broken you and you let it build you up. Even if you didn't want that strength at the beginning, you've got it now. You give me hope for a better future." That hint of insecurity bubbled to the surface, tainting her words with doubt.

She shouldn't doubt herself. If anything, I should be thanking her for never giving up on me, even when I didn't believe in myself. I wasn't usually a hugger, but I pulled her to me and held tight. She stiffened in my embrace, like she wasn't used to people giving her affection. I wondered how she could have faith in me but so little in herself. But that was a question for another day, because the front doors opened and Hutton stalked out, followed by the woman who'd brought me down from the infirmary.

"That's my cue. Good luck," Kelsey whispered as she extricated herself from my embrace and fell into line behind Hutton.

I watched them traipse through the gates and caught the councilman's eye. I intended to keep my word this summer. No matter what happened to me, I wasn't going to let him screw over other people, even if I wasn't wholly convinced they deserved it. What was the point of having convictions if you didn't stick to them? I turned to see Dean Bevan watching me. Our gazes met and I could have sworn I saw a glimmer of gratitude in them before he pivoted and disappeared back inside.

Chapter Twenty-Four

I'd barely left the dorm after they'd taken Celine and the others away. Even though I hadn't shown my face around the grounds, I knew that everyone was talking about me, anyway. They were all whispering about the druid plot to steal our magic and how I'd stopped it. Of course, no one seemed interested in the fact Celine had tried to overthrow the dean. Even he seemed to have glossed over that fact.

"Even if you aren't going out, you could at least shower," Eva commented from across the room.

She'd at least been venturing out to get food for me. She'd been indulging my self-imposed quarantine, but I could read on her face she thought it was getting old.

"I don't smell that bad," I grumbled before taking a sniff. Okay, yeah, I could use a shower. "On second thought, maybe the hot water would do me good."

"People out there aren't mad at you, Nor. They're impressed," she told me as I rooted through my non-uniform clothes. It was nice to be able to wear whatever I wanted now that the semester was over. In a few short days we'd have our exam results and I'd know whether I would be coming back in September...or not.

"They don't even know what happened. It wasn't like I single-handedly took on two enforcers. I had help."

More than I wanted to admit because that meant I had to acknowledge that Celine played a part, and then I'd turned her in. "My point is, they don't know everything, and that just makes it speculation. I've had enough of that in my life, thank you very much."

"I think it's more that people see that you have worth and it makes you uncomfortable," Eva said as she passed me a towel.

"I don't like being centre of attention," I mumbled.

"I know. Believe me, I know that. But whether you like it or not, you stopped them from ruining a lot of lives. You deserve the praise they're giving you."

"But not everyone is heaping on praise, Eva. People who believe Celine is worth following think I screwed her over." I still felt responsible for sending her to prison, even if it was only six weeks. But at least she'd still have her powers at the end of things.

I'd been willing to go along with her plan for a while. Just because I turned on her didn't absolve me of that guilt. I knew Eva would tell me that I only went along in the end to stop the plan. That I shouldn't feel responsible because I didn't put the plan in their heads. I didn't force them to do anything they didn't want. And if I hadn't gone along with them, I wouldn't have known about the druid plan.

"You're being broody," she sighed.

"Seems to be my new state of being," I replied.

"Well, go explore that new state of being in the bloody shower." She made a shooing motion toward the door, and I took the hint.

Climbing into the shower five minutes later felt amazing. Using all that magic had worn me out and I was still recovering, magically speaking. The healers said I would be for a while. I hadn't even been able to conjure a simple bolt of electricity in days. But the hot water pounding on my neck and back rejuvenated me in a way hiding under the covers hadn't.

By the time I stepped out of the bathroom, I felt like a human being again. One who might even venture beyond the door to her dormitory. I checked the room to find it empty. There was no note to suggest where my roommate had gone, but that was fine. I could wander by myself.

I stopped at the stairs leading down to the first floor and up to the cursed floor. Apparently, after everything that went down, no one was stupid enough to venture upstairs. They didn't want to end up punching their ticket to prison. I turned and made my way down to the ground floor.

Given how much runes had played into what Seneca and Bryden had been doing, I couldn't help scanning every surface for them. They didn't look to be active now, but they were still there. If the Circle was telling the truth, they'd be gone by the new semester. I'd be keeping a close eye on that. They had a lot to prove in my book. The fact they'd had people acting with such malicious intent under their noses was worrying at best.

"Norah." His voice made me stop dead in my tracks.

I didn't want to turn around in case I'd imagined it. But then there was a soft gust of air that brushed past my face, and when I did turn, it was to see Zachary standing there in his enforcer's uniform beneath a black-trimmed red cloak. His left palm glowed a pale yellow. I wanted to run to him and throw my arms around him. Or punch him for abandoning me. Or maybe just kiss him for hours. *Why were guys so damn complicated?*

"You're still here," I finally replied, without moving from my spot.

He stepped up beside me, shoving his hands into the pockets of his trousers. "I was hoping I could apologise."

"You don't have to be sorry for anything. I shouldn't have kissed you. I get that. You made it very clear how you felt."

"That's the thing, no I didn't. Yes, you caught me off guard. And I knew it wouldn't be well-received by my commanders if they heard I was involved with a student."

"Right, boundaries."

"And I won't lie. Even if they managed to get past the

thought of me seeing a student, the fact it was you would have rankled them beyond belief."

I turned to face him and cocked my head to one side. "Is this how you imagined your apology going in your head? Because you're quite rubbish at it."

He smiled and ducked his head. "No."

He exhaled slowly and his hands made an appearance, reaching for mine. "I said all that because I am sorry that I let what other people would think of me get I the way of how I feel. I like you, Norah. And given that kiss, I'm pretty sure you like me, too."

"Yeah, well, maybe a little less now that you've ghosted me all semester."

"I was busy. And, it seems, so were you."

"What are you talking about?"

"I know you stopped Seneca and Brayden. After Valentine's Day, I knew something was off. I had cleared that corridor myself. I knew it was clear. So something else was going on. I talked to the other enforcers and none of them had any trouble with that area after I cleared it."

"You knew what they were doing, and you just did nothing?"

"I didn't know exactly what they were doing. They may be less experienced than me, but that doesn't make them stupider. They were covering their tracks. By the time I realised they were using runes, you were in the middle of your exams."

"You left the note with the stone chip in my bag?"

He blushed. "I'd seen you and Seneca blow up eat each other enough to know she was targeting you. I didn't know what she had planned for the runes exactly, but I knew it wasn't good. And I didn't want you to get hurt if I could help it."

"The Circle said they're sending hex breakers in over the summer to clean up their mess."

"So I heard. And I'm being called back to the Circle for reassignment after this semester. So, uh, maybe we could stay in touch. If you aren't too pissed at me for ghosting you."

"It wouldn't break any rules?"

"Well, it won't matter who I'm seeing if I'm not assigned here."

My heart was screaming that yes, I'd like to see him. That it would be nice to have a boyfriend. But there was still the possibility I'd end up back in the real world with no powers at all. Would he want me then?

"What if I fail and they kick me out?"

"You won't fail out," he said.

"But what if I do? What then? Would you like come visit me on weekends or whatever at my parents' place?"

"Wherever you wanted."

"I don't know if I'm really ready for something serious." And my intuition told me Zachary would be serious as a heart attack.

"Fair enough. You've had a lot going on this past year. How about this, I'll give you a way to stay in touch and if you feel like chatting or hanging out, let me know. No pressure. I'm around if you're up for it."

"Thanks." After a pause, I asked, "Why are you so confident I'm not getting expelled?"

"Well, I mean, it would be pretty poor form to expel the student who saved the academy. Besides, I saw Instructor Glover a little while ago and she said that they'd be posting exam results later today. I may have got a little peek at her exams and saw you passed."

Before I could head off to the lecture rooms corridor—I didn't want to check my results with the masses—Zachary caught my hand in his, spun me around and kissed me. It was slow and sweet. His body pressed gently against mine, the only hint of something more. I didn't want it to end, and I couldn't hide my disappointment when he stepped back.

"Thanks for sneaking a peek for me," I murmured.

"I knew you'd be worried, so I figured I could bring a little good news." He brushed his lips across the back of my knuckles. "I'll see you around, Norah."

My heart thumped an erratic two-step all the way to

the lecture room corridor. Someone must have tipped off Rory because he was standing in front of Weaver's door when I got there. It was strange to see the space so empty or him without his own entourage. I almost turned around, but he spotted me.

"You get the word they'd gone up, too?"

"Yeah. I heard. I guess I wasn't the only one who wanted to see my fate before everyone else knew."

He gave me a small, sheepish grin. "Me, too."

"You? Come on. I'm sure you did brilliant," I offered. Even if he was an oaf a lot of the time, he was still a person with feelings.

"Not really. People assume because I'm big, I must be dumb. And sometimes I feel like I really am. The words don't always make sense, you know?"

"Yeah, but most of these classes you don't need to read," I said.

"More than half we did," he said. "And written exams were never my thing."

He was worried about the same thing as me. I didn't have his fear of not knowing what things said, but I felt just as subpar with my skills. "Well, how about this? I'll check for you and you check for me. That way neither of us is alone."

"That sounds good," he said, and started running his finger down the sheet of printed names. "Looks like you scored an Acceptable."

"Shut up, I did not." I shoved him aside to read the list. Sure enough, there was an Acceptable printed next to my name. Eva's, too. "I thought for sure I'd flunk this one. Shadows and plants aren't exactly friends. That plant was half-dead when I left."

"What'd I get?" His voice shook.

I scanned for his name. "Oh, you didn't do too bad. Got an Acceptable as well."

He let out a long breath. "That's one down. I'm pretty sure I passed Rathbone's exam."

"Me, too. How about we save that for last… end on a good note, right?"

"Yeah. Good thinking."

We went from lecture room to lecture room, checking for each other's names. With each passing list, my heart hammered a little faster. And on each subject, I got an Acceptable. Some were even Goods. Somehow, despite everything, I'd passed every subject. Rory, too, even if it was just barely in some. And Eva, of course, had aced the whole lot, putting the pair of us to shame. But who cared? A pass was a pass.

"So, I guess this means both of us are going into second year," I said as we stood by Rathbone's lecture room.

"Yeah. Look, uh, I'm sorry I was kind of a prat to you

all year. I shouldn't have assumed you were dangerous just because of your family."

"You weren't the only one, so don't worry about it."

"Well, uh, I guess I'll see you around next semester."

He jogged off and left me standing there in silence. Today was shaping up to be full of apologies. I couldn't imagine who else would pop out of the woodwork now to offer up a *mea culpa* next. Instead, the door to Rathbone's office opened, and he appeared in the doorway.

"Shit, were you in there the whole time?" I said, then realised I'd just cursed in front of an instructor and kicked myself.

"Don't worry, I'm not going to rat you or Rory out. I am glad I ran into you, though. I wanted to tell you how impressed I was with your exam results. You really applied yourself. And don't go spreading it around, but you were one of the only students to get it on their first go."

"Thanks." I dug my toe into a crack in the stone flooring in front of me, trying to hide the heat of embarrassment rising up the tips of my ears. I really needed to work on accepting praise. "This is going to sound so cheesy, but you were the first person to be nice to me here. Thanks for that."

"Everyone deserves to be judged on their own merits,

Norah. You are no different. You are going to become a fine young witch, of that I have no doubt."

He clapped me on the shoulder. "And I hope to see you in my Runes class come next semester. Something tells me you're going to be great at it."

"I'll be there. And thanks again for believing in me."

"Good. Now, I think someone is waiting for you."

He opened the door fully, and I saw Eva inside. I frowned, and she shot me a grin.

"What? Didn't think I was going to hold your hand the whole time you snuck around checking your results, did you? I mean, not after I checked them all myself, that is."

I laughed and grabbed her in a hug.

"You're a sneaky little witch," I told her.

"Right back at you, Nor."

"So...second year." I exhaled slowly. "That's a thing."

"Yes," she agreed, "It is. Told you that you could do it."

Until now, I hadn't realised how much I wanted to be back here come September and how much this was beginning to feel like a safe place—druid attacks and attempted coups notwithstanding, that was.

It had been far from a perfect year, but I was starting to find where I fit, here and in the world. And sure, there were a lot of druids out there who still thought of me and the rest of the unclassifieds as lesser beings, but there were others, like Kelsey, who wanted us to be equal. What was that saying about being the change we wanted to see in the world? I'd started off this journey wanting to make people listen and I'd definitely achieved that goal, even if it hadn't been the way I'd intended. I'd achieved other goals, too—ones I hadn't even known had mattered to me, like making friends. People like Eva, who I couldn't imagine life without. And unlikely allies, like Kelsey, who would be there if I needed her. And then there was Zachary—whatever he was to me now—and I found that I couldn't wait to discover where that led.

I had begun this year wishing there was some way I could make the magic inside me go away. But my shadow magic wasn't a curse, or something to be thrown away lightly. It was a part of me, a part I'd been afraid to embrace. They say that fear never makes a good decision, and maybe they're right. I have a feeling that next year, I'm going to get plenty of chances to find out.

But right now, in the halls of the second home I hadn't been seeking, with a friend I didn't know I'd needed, I was content. Happy. More than that, I was Shadow Charmed.

A note from the authors

Thanks for joining us for Norah's first year at the Braeseth Academy of Unclassified Magic. We hope you enjoyed it as much as we did! Be sure to come back for her second year in Shadow Cursed, book 2 in the Misfit Magic Academy series. Order it from Amazon by scanning the QR code below:

Printed in Great Britain
by Amazon

85706061R00173